She wondered
If Frank would be alone

The flight to Nassau had tired Laura, but she had to see the man she loved and apologize for accusing him of being involved with Julie Schell. She should have known it wasn't true.

She rang the doorbell. A muted tinkle sounded inside, and for a moment she heard nothing else. The sound of the surf was clearly audible from beyond the house. Maybe Frank was out on the beach.

At last she heard soft steps approaching. The latch came loose, and the door opened slowly. Laura's heart nearly stopped. Julie Schell stood before her, clad only in a man's bathrobe, her delicate eyebrows arched.

"Miss Christensen," she said calmly. "What a surprise. Do come in."

Books by Donna Huxley

HARLEQUIN PRESENTS
754—INTIMATE
776—NUMBER ONE
792—A STRANGER TO LOVE

These books may be available at your local bookseller.

DONNA HUXLEY

a stranger to love

Harlequin Books

TORONTO • NEW YORK • LONDON
AMSTERDAM • PARIS • SYDNEY • HAMBURG
STOCKHOLM • ATHENS • TOKYO • MILAN

Harlequin Presents first edition June 1985
ISBN 0-373-10792-7

Original hardcover edition published in 1984
by Mills & Boon Limited

PROLOGUE

THE young woman lay in darkness, her sandy-coloured hair splayed in soft billows across the spread which covered her naked body. The gentle curve of her breasts rose and fell soundlessly as she slept. In repose her fine features bore a childlike innocence, dominated as they were by the long lashes over her closed eyes.

A tiny tremor shook the slender fingers of her resting hand in the silence. The creamy flesh of her brow furrowed in an unconscious frown, and then softened as the dream thought passed.

In her dream she was back home with Mother and Dad. But the house on Everit Street did not resemble itself. The rooms were larger, darker, more melancholy.

A party was going on. The guests were all dressed in white. It was as though they were functionaries of some sort, the bland uniformity of their garb bespeaking the nature of their trade. A host of milkmen, perhaps, or ice-cream men gathered for an occult purpose which Mother and Dad seemed to understand quite well.

Dad introduced Laura around. The men smiled down at her as they held out their tanned hands. Their expressions were sympathetic and yet somehow implacable.

Then she was on a train which roared along gleaming rails past landscapes she had never seen before. Outside the window she could see people going about their business on horseback, or pushing little carts along the dirt paths. They tilled fields where

5

fruits glowed like rich candy under the golden sun. She was lost, and must find her way to a station where she might change trains.

But the train showed no sign of stopping. Instead it gained speed, taking Laura further and further from home. The tunnel was approaching with fearsome urgency, like a predator whose quick jaws would close over its victim, ineluctable and cruel. The car hurtled forward, its violent flight making her dizzy. In a moment she must surely slip from her seat and cling in terror to the hard floor of the careening carriage, as though otherwise she would be flung into space by the sheer force of it all . . .

Her eyes opened with a start. For a moment the soft obscurity around her seemed to rock and heave with the ghost of the leaping train. Then all was still, and her eyes began to close.

The hushed intimacy of the soft spread against her breasts and thighs told her she was naked. Dreamily she wondered what had become of her nightgown. The grey light of dawn shone pale across a ceiling which was not that of her bedroom in New Haven. The muted city sounds outside were not those that greeted her on weekday mornings when she reached to turn off the alarm moments before it rang.

The rooms of her lifetime wheeled slowly through her imagination, seeking to adjust themselves to the walls she now felt around her. She recalled the bedroom she had occupied as a child on Everit Street, and her dorm room at college. Out of nowhere loomed the cabin she had lived in at summer camp, with its hard wood floor and the scent of pine needles and campfires to which she had awakened on fresh summer mornings.

For a long somnolent moment she watched with pleasure as her familiar rooms paraded before her in a silent panorama.

Then, with a little start of terror, she remembered she was not alone.

Everything came into focus with jarring suddenness. No wonder, she thought, her sleeping mind had tried to transport her to a familiar place. The quiet room hovering around her was indeed strange. She had never seen it before last night. And the city outside had been nothing more than an image in a hundred travel books until yesterday.

No wonder, indeed, that she hesitated to turn her eyes to the sleeping man beside her. She had never shared his bed before.

Holding her body still, she listened for the sound of his breathing. It was barely perceptible, calm and regular.

The taste of his skin was still on her lips. Every corner of her body bore the trace of his touch, and of his clean virile scent. Her senses, dulled by sleep, began to awaken to their own memory of his hard body.

Now he slept peacefully. But a few short hours ago he had been a storm of pleasure around and inside her, unimaginable in its intimacy. The flesh of her breasts quickened anew as images of softly probing lips and hands hung tauntingly before her mind's eye. The naked limbs luxuriating under this warm coverlet tingled still from the caresses which had teased them into a fever of wanting. Delighted to have been known so totally, inflamed to so perfect a height of excitement, her traitorous body slumbered in the glow of its satisfaction, indifferent to the scruples haunting her mind.

She blushed from head to toe in the shadows.

It was all too plain now. The unreal landscape of her dream seemed haggard and pathetic now that wakefulness had shorn it of its fascination.

Well might she resuscitate Mother and Dad in her sleeping mind, she reflected bitterly. They were both dead and gone now. The house on Everit Street was sold. She was alone now, a woman on her own and in charge of her existence.

To the outside world she was Laura Christensen, president and majority stockholder of one of the largest corporations in New England. Only six weeks ago the business press had teemed with speculative items about the responsibility thrust upon her, and about the fate of her company.

They were all watching in curiosity to see what she would do. Investors, executives, journalists, competitors . . . All eyes were upon Laura, and she could feel their speculation, their scepticism, their indifferent interest. Would Christensen Products retain its precarious position of strength in a recession economy? Or would its young president show herself incapable of steering it on the right course?

The *Wall Street Journal* had somehow got hold of her college yearbook picture and printed it alongside the brief account of her accession to the presidency of the company. She had cringed to see her youthful image published for all to see. Though four years had passed since the photo was taken, Laura could not deny that the face she saw in the mirror each morning retained its girlish vitality.

Would the *Journal*'s readers—cunning entrepreneurs and bankers, alert investors and brokers—draw the right conclusion from the picture of callow youth displayed on its back page? Would they quickly understand that a major company had fallen into the hands of a silly schoolgirl?

For this morning such was precisely Laura's concept of herself. A silly young girl, well out of her element in the cut-throat business community of the East Coast. An inexperienced junior executive thrust into a limelight she could neither cope with nor escape.

At last she dared to turn her eyes to the sleeping man beside her. His black hair was tousled by his night's repose, but also by the impassioned caress of Laura's own heedless fingers last night. The strong lines of his hard face were softened now by sleep, but when he awoke his ebony irises would scan the world around him with their alert gleam.

Sheepishly Laura glanced at his long, powerful limbs, at the square shoulders above his deep chest. All that had been hers last night. And she had been his.

She barely knew this enigmatic man. Yet, within the dizzy space of six weeks, he had made himself indispensable to her. Underneath his harsh, demanding exterior she had thought she saw the shade of a tenderness for her and a sympathy for her plight. She had clung to that shade without daring to question its reality. After all, was she not the plaything of the storm of events that had engulfed her? Should she not be grateful that he had taken pity on her in her extremity, and agreed to marshal the daunting resources of his intelligence and expertise in her behalf, when his instincts must surely dictate that he leave her to her fate and seek his fortune elsewhere?

Yet she cursed her helpless dependence no less than the insidious desire that had inflamed her towards Frank Jordan. Had he not providentially joined the company only a month before the cataclysm which left it in Laura's unsure hands, disaster might already have resulted. It was thanks to the unflappable confidence behind Frank's penetrating eyes that Christensen Products retained its fighting chance for survival. No one saw his picture in the *Journal*, but it was Frank whose initiative had kept the company afloat until now, and his guile and courage remained the key to its future.

Gratefully Laura had accepted his counsel and followed his recommendations, for she knew she had no choice.

And now she had given herself to him.

A wry smile of dismay curled her lips in the silence, for she knew her shame went deeper yet. For weeks she had awaited the charmed moment when he would catch the signals her woman's body sought to attract him with. And when it had finally happened, here in this alien room in a strange city, she had been his eager partner, her sighs of rapture indicating her delight and relief that, in this way as well, he had taken pity on her.

She was all open to him now, defenceless and dependent. She dared not imagine the thoughts which might lurk behind his inscrutable irises when he awoke to find her here. She must hope against hope that, whatever his contempt for her, he would find it in his heart to go on as before; that his newfound loyalty to the company Sam Christensen had spent a lifetime building would outstrip his scorn for the behaviour of Sam's heedless daughter.

His powerful body stirred beside her, and was still once more. A lock of his dark hair had fallen across the strong brow over the angular contours of his face. Even in sleep he seemed vital, alert as an athlete coiled for action.

In a few moments more his eyes would open. He would remember everything, and know exactly what it all meant—for Frank Jordan always knew where he stood. In six weeks Laura had learned to admire that sharp gaze which scanned the world of men like a clear beacon, calculating, evaluating, knowing. She prayed it would still rest upon her with its spark of friendliness, and lead her through the labyrinth in which her company was mired.

She had cast her lot with him, and must trust him now. For without Frank Jordan she was surely lost.

To think that three months ago he had had no existence for her at all! She had been a bright, cheerful young woman pursuing an orderly career, without a thought for the fragility of her sunlit life.

The rabbit runs free in the fields, she recalled an old parable, *and the hounds play in the courtyard. But the rabbit's fate is already sealed.* Thus it had been for Laura as well.

And now the hounds were upon her.

In another minute he would be awake. She must look ahead, imagine what he would say and do. Try to predict whether things would be changed between them, and whether he would still stand between her and the things she could not control.

But it was no use. As she lay numb in her nudity, in these last moments of silence, the future was as unknowable as ever.

She could only recall how it had all started, and wonder again at the twisting whirlwind of happenings that had uprooted her so suddenly from her careless past.

CHAPTER ONE

'LAURA, I want to make you a Vice-President of Christensen as of the first of the year.'

Sam Christensen smiled with a touch of irony at his daughter's pursed lips and furrowed brow. He knew what her response would be.

'Dad,' Laura smiled at last, shaking her head in amused disapproval, 'do we have to start this again? I'm happy just where I am. If you give me more responsibility, you'll turn me into the same sort of workaholic the company has made of you. Is that what you want?'

'That's not what I want, and it's not going to happen,' Sam said, his husky voice bubbling with its accustomed energy. 'I own the company. I have a right to be overprotective about it and to work long hours. Your mother understood that, and so have you. But if you're suggesting that I overwork my executives . . .'

Ruefully Laura smiled her admiration for Sam's famous talent at argument and cajolery.

'There you go, putting words in my mouth again,' she said. 'I didn't say your high-level people aren't happy. But they will be more than a little annoyed when they see an inexperienced nobody like me elevated to a position on par with their own. They're experts, Dad. I'm only a novice at this business.'

'Well, now,' Sam said with a theatrical gesture of hurt pride. 'First she tells me I'm a slavedriver, and now she claims I don't know better than to hire incompetent executives.'

'Dad!' Laura returned, her patience wearing thin.

'Please don't be this way. If you need more help in Research, why don't you simply find someone truly competent and hire him—or her? There are experienced people all over the country who would love to come to work for you.'

Sam Christensen shook his head slowly as he twirled the empty wine glass in his hand. Even in her exasperation at his stubbornness Laura had to admire his vitality. The small brown eyes looking out from beneath his thick brows were alive with a sparkling urgency from which a touch of humour was never absent. The hint of grey at his temples only served to accentuate the youthful thickness of his sandy-coloured hair. Everyone said Sam looked twenty years younger than his age, and Laura herself was often disconcerted by his energy. After a long day spent in the busy workshops of Christensen Products' research division, she felt so drained that her father's buoyant high spirits seemed nothing short of superhuman.

The company was his life's blood, and had been for the last thirty years. From its first halting steps in the turbulent business world of the East Coast to its present status as a major producer of precision industrial parts and small appliances, Christensen Products had been Sam's vocation and avocation combined. With a zest that daunted his competitors and assured the fidelity of his employees, Sam watched over the company, now expanding its capacities, now cutting back, now pioneering a new product, now struggling with a faltering market. He was the company's mother hen and cheerful master of ceremonies, and his every executive move bespoke more than a mere ambition for growth or success. It was genuine love for his vulnerable, growing creation that motivated him, as each bright young executive he hired soon learned.

Sam's profit-sharing arrangement with his employees was considered revolutionary when he first instituted it over a generation ago. His experiments with four-day work weeks and innovative retirement programmes had the experts in Personnel scratching their heads in befuddlement—until the resulting increases in Christensen's productivity forced them to acknowledge his genius for getting the most out of his workers.

With the passing years Sam had become a legendary figure in the business community. When his wife died as he was approaching retirement age it was assumed that he would finally hand over the reins of his company to one of his trusted lieutenants, and content himself with a place on his own Board of Directors. But Sam surprised everyone, including Laura, by throwing himself into his work with more eagerness than ever.

'I've promised my daughter I'll retire and take it easy,' ran his oft-quoted statement in a New York business magazine's admiring profile, '—as soon as she reaches the age of sixty-five.'

Indeed, only Sam's protective concern for his daughter seemed a more urgent consideration than his own future. After her mother's death he found time for regular visits to the large university where Laura was completing her degree in engineering. Though he kept his own grief in a private corner of his personality, he spoke with touching intuition of the pain such a loss can bring to a young woman starting out in life.

'Death is not a welcome guest, Laura,' she recalled his grave and realistic words. 'You've got to feel bad. Your mother would have expected you to. But she would also want you to bury your loss, keep her in your memory, and start living again. You go back to your work now, and show those professor types what you're made of. One of these mornings you'll wake up feeling good again.'

At the time Laura had accepted her father's kindly support and reassurance without a second thought. Today, when she looked back on those painful times, she could not find words to express her gratitude for the sacrifices Sam had made on her behalf. Though a busy and influential businessman whose company was rapidly becoming a small empire, he would appear on campus to take her to dinner, to a movie or concert, for all the world as though he had no obligations which could compete with his pride in his daughter's academic achievements.

Upon her graduation Sam offered Laura a position in his company.

'We like to interview as many promising young people as we can,' he said with a straight face. 'Of course, with your qualifications, you'll want to consider other possibilities, other companies perhaps. But I think I can promise you an exciting outlet for your talents at Christensen Products. Naturally your own decision will be final, and whatever you choose will be fine with me.'

With new eyes Laura studied the Research Division she had occasionally visited as a curious schoolgirl. Sam Christensen was an inventor at heart, and never shrank from investing time and money in exciting product ideas and the people who refined them—even if the time for such products had not yet come in the uncertain economy of the moment. Laura's college education had equipped her to contribute creatively to product development, and she could see opportunities for a rapid increase in her own knowledge through work at Christensen.

Still, Laura wondered whether she should go to work for her own father. The idea came as a surprise, for Sam had never mentioned it during her high school or college years.

Her decision was made for her when she studied the

finely tuned interrelationships of all the divisions at Christensen's New Haven headquarters. While working in research Laura would be able to learn all there was to know about materials, test marketing, design and manufacture. Rather than languish in an isolated corner of the corporation, she could follow each new product from its birth on the design table or computer display to its final role in a modern factory or consumer household.

Finally, Laura was impressed by the camaraderie and high spirits of her father's employees. From the line workers to the highest executives, they admired and trusted Sam Christensen. What was more, they seemed delighted with the prospect of working with Laura, and no one hinted at the slightest resentment of her.

It was too happy and stimulating a situation to refuse. One month after her college graduation Laura came to work in New Haven. With Sam's agreement she found a comfortable apartment at a convenient distance from work. Sam continued to occupy the stately house on Everit Street.

'You'll feel better on your own,' he said. 'You're an independent young woman now, and there's no reason for you to be tied to your old man's house. Besides,' he added with his wry smile, 'the wild parties at my place would keep you from getting your sleep.'

In the four years since that happy beginning, Laura's ideas about her professional future had changed radically. No longer content to pursue her original plan of working exclusively in engineering, she began to look forward to the distant day when she might run her own small business. Perhaps, she reflected, something of Sam's proprietary tenderness for his own products had rubbed off on her. More and more she imagined herself working closely with a team of business professionals to create and market innovative consumer products. One day she would control a modest company of her own, and would be familiar with every detail of its operations. To watch such an enterprise grow under her own care would be a dream come true.

Sam must have sensed this budding ambition in his daughter, for his sparkling eyes rested proudly on her as he answered her eager questions about Christensen Products' complex financial structure during their regular dinners together. But as time passed Laura realised there was an ulterior motive behind his encouragement. Sam shared her dream that she might one day control her own company. But he wanted that company to be Christensen Products. What was more, his timetable for Laura's rise to top-level executive responsibility was far more ambitious than her own.

Today's lighthearted argument was merely the latest skirmish in a quiet battle which had been going on between father and daughter for over two years. Laura was not at all convinced that her relatively limited experience in research qualified her for so challenging a position as Vice-President. Nor was she sure that her sudden rise in rank would please the employees with whom she had worked on such friendly terms. Given the choice, she knew she might well prefer to remain prudently ensconced among her creative, somewhat excitable research colleagues, and to confine her ambition to lobbying Sam for the manufacture of certain new products which remained at the prototype stage. Chief among these was an ingenious portable dust filtration system designed by a Christensen engineer named Randy Powers. The unique sensitivity of the filter Randy had invented permitted the little machine to virtually eliminate dust throughout several rooms of a house or apartment.

Laura's cost analyses had convinced her that the device could be marketed at an affordable price. But

Sam insisted that in the depressed economy of the day its immediate production would be too great a risk against projected profits. Through continuing cajolery and thorough marketing projections Laura hoped to change his mind.

Now, as she contemplated Sam's plump body and expectant eyes, Laura had no inkling that her choices were about to run out.

'Dad,' she said, 'you have your own contacts. Why don't you find someone who is truly qualified for this job? Someone who is already respected in his field . . . like Frank Jordan.'

The name slipped out before Laura could suppress it. Only a month ago Frank Jordan, a top executive in the New York headquarters of the enormous Schell International conglomerate, had delighted Sam by agreeing to join Christensen Products. Jordan's reputation as an expert manager and financial analyst had preceded him and, on the few occasions when she found herself in his presence, Laura had decided that his arrogance more than matched his reputed abilities.

'Frank Jordan?' Sam shrugged. 'He's a special case. He's trained for a bigger pond than Christensen, but he simply got sick and tired of all the red tape in that Schell behemoth. He likes our products, and we're lucky to have him. But he's a troubleshooter rather than a specialist.'

Troublemaker is more like it, Laura thought ruefully. The memory of Jordan's sharp, piercing eyes and roguish demeanor had irked her since their first meeting. Though he stopped short of real condescension towards Sam's executives, Frank seemed sceptical of nearly all the business concepts they took for granted. After listening with an air of calm evaluation to the proposals of others, he would respond with laconic, pitilessly analytical remarks which bespoke a colossal self-confidence to match his highly original business mind. Laura could not help suspecting that Jordan, who was rumoured to have been a trusted confidant of the great Armand Schell himself, considered himself to be slumming in a mid-sized company like Christensen Products.

Her impression was hardly diminished by the ill-concealed mockery of the glances he shot her way. Uncomfortably she wondered whether he was pigeon-holing her as the spoiled corporate daughter whose abilities did not justify her position. And she was more than a little daunted by the aggressive and even ruthless view of marketing tactics to which he was implacably committed. To judge by the hard, handsome lines of his tanned face, he was a man in his mid-thirties who had already tasted so much power and success that he was pleased to lower his personal sights for Sam's sake. Yet his demeanour suggested so boundless an ambition that Laura could not under-stand why he had not sought a company presidency for himself.

'Perhaps Jordan is not the best example,' she admitted. 'But the business world is full of experts, Dad. I'm only a beginner.'

'Laura,' Sam sighed, 'on one point only I'll agree that you are inexperienced. That point is hiring. I've been moving this company along for thirty years now, and I've hired and fired a lot of high management people. I've learned one thing from my experience: you've got to fill your responsible positions with people who *care* about the company, over and above their ability to do the work. I can spot that quality a mile away, and smell out its absence just as easily. You have the dedication I want and need, Laura. You're not in this business just to buy yourself a house with a swimming pool. You want to learn and to contribute. Now, give your old man credit for some old-fashioned good sense. I want you to take over Research because I know I can count on you to do the job for this company.'

'And if I failed?' Laura asked quietly.

'That's impossible,' he shook his head. 'I know what you're made of, Laura.'

Sam seemed to have tired suddenly. His ruddy cheeks had gone slack, and he touched his forehead with an unsteady hand.

'Dad, let's not talk about this any more now,' Laura said.

'Where's Mary?' Sam frowned. 'Tell her to get me an aspirin, would you, honey? I've got the damndest headache.'

'I'll get it myself.' Pushing back her chair Laura hurried from the dining room. Sam's one concession to his doctor's orders was the large bottle of aspirins in his upstairs medicine cabinet. He took one tablet per day in accordance with the current theory that the drug's anti-coagulant properties might provide insurance against circulatory troubles.

Laura shook two tablets into her palm and started down the stairs. The twang of a fallen glass against silverware in the dining room below made her hurry her steps.

Sam was staring into space, his expression wan and depressed. Laura had never seen such sad preoccupation in his sparkling eyes. His water glass lay on its side on the tablecloth.

'Dad?' Laura approached him, alarmed by the sudden change in his demeanour.

But before she could place a hand on his shoulder he exhaled sharply, gasped, and fell forward, his face on the table top.

'Dad!' Laura cried in confusion. 'Mary!'

The colour was beginning to leave the unconscious man's cheeks. Laura grasped his wrist, touched his neck, and saw her own tears fall on his shoulder.

'Mary! Call an ambulance. Hurry! I think he's had a heart attack.'

Desperately Laura fought to recall the resuscitation techniques she had learned while a college student. She pulled her father's inert body to the floor. The pupils of his staring eyes were dilated, immobile. To her horror there was no pulse.

Time seemed to curl upon itself and disappear like a fold in a curtain as she pressed at the burly chest beneath her, for in a trice white-shirted men were pulling her away from her father and shouting orders to each other as they worked on his motionless form. Underneath the plastic mask covering his mouth and nose, Sam Christensen seemed even less himself. His blue face was neither sad nor happy. It was adamant, stubborn, empty.

Laura knew then that he was already dead.

She rode with him in the ambulance, banished to a corner of the vehicle by the busy paramedics. Bleakly she followed his stretcher to the emergency room, and stood unseeing as the doctors extended its aluminum legs and moved him to a heavy table.

No one thought to force her to leave as a resident, barking commands to his team, forced a syringe into Sam's chest. Everyone moved so quickly, Laura thought without hope. The body jumped like a marionnette attached to unseen strings as the electrodes sent shocks through the gel smeared over its chest.

For what seemed an eternity the struggle to revive Sam continued, punctuated by grunted, irritable words of encouragement and exhortation from the doctors. As their science reached its limits, they called to Dad, importuned him to wake up, pleaded with him.

It had taken ten minutes. Sam Christensen was prounounced Dead on Arrival at Yale-New Haven Hospital at 7:21 p.m., November 9th. The cause of his death, as written on the certificate mailed to Laura three days later, was a massive stroke.

CHAPTER TWO

'I'M afraid we can't help you any longer,' Andrew Dillon said coolly from behind his enormous executive desk. 'First Federal's policies on corporate debt may seem inflexible, but without them we would go bankrupt ourselves. Your company is in arrears on sixty million dollars' worth of short-term debt, Miss Christensen, and most of those notes will come due within the next six to seven months. First Federal simply can't carry Christensen Products on those terms.'

Through the haze of her anxiety Laura noticed Andrew Dillon's coldly efficient demeanor. He was all business—there was no doubt of that. The cup of coffee he had decorously poured for Laura now sat untouched by her side, its steaming warmth having vanished along with her hopes. Still vital in his late middle age, Andrew Dillon looked down upon her through grey eyes under his immaculately tonsured white hair. Behind him the Manhattan skyline gleamed under the bright November sun outside the First Federal Bank's enormous headquarters.

As President of the bank, Andrew Dillon was responsible for every transaction going on in the hundreds of offices throughout this building, and in branches all over New England. Lulled at first by his gentle urbanity, Laura had come to realise that it concealed his banker's interest in his own institution's prosperity—at whatever cost in indifference and even cruelty towards those beholden to him.

'I . . . I don't understand how this could have happened so suddenly,' Laura stammered. 'I'm sure . . .'

'I think you'd have to discuss that with your own accounting people,' Mr Dillon interrupted. 'I know your father was perfectly aware that Christensen was on the brink of an urgent financial situation. However, he did not apprise us of his intentions in the matter. With Sam Christensen dead, sad as the situation is, the bank really has no alternative.'

Laura reddened to hear the note of condescension in his voice. Clearly he believed that Christensen Products was an unacceptable risk for his bank since the demise of its dynamic founder.

'What do you suggest?' Laura asked evenly.

'Well.' Andrew Dillon moved slightly in his chair and placed his elbows on the desk before him. Laura thought she sensed a trace of animation in him at last. 'There are of course many options which you'll want to discuss with your own people. Bankruptcy is one.' He pronounced the word without a hint of hesitation or sympathy.

'Bankruptcy?' Laura exclaimed in shock. 'You can't mean that.'

'As I say, it's one option. Bankruptcy would allow you the retention of a fraction of the company's assets while satisfying your creditors. The other major option, of course, is a merger. This is somewhat more problematic, since you'd have to find a corporation large enough to absorb your debt. However, I think there is a chance in this direction.'

'What chance?' Her head spinning, Laura fought to concentrate her attention on his every word.

'First Federal has some minor dealings, for instance, with Schell International's American division. Of my knowledge I am aware that Schell has an interest in some of the markets your father has developed over the years. I don't know if they have any intention of acting on that now, of course. Multinational corporations like Schell are unpredictable. Sometimes they make decisions virtually overnight, and sometimes they take months or even years. Nevertheless, Schell seems to me a good bet for you.'

For years the financial publications Laura read had been full of news of the enormous Schell Corporation. Its subsidiaries spanned the world, and for twenty years its stock had grown steadily in value. Christensen Products, despite its own large size and importance to the economy of the East Coast, was a mere corporate midget compared to the Schell empire.

Yet Laura recalled that the business press rarely spoke of Schell's recent dealings with real admiration. The comglomerate's reputation as an innovative manufacturing and construction entity seemed to have tarnished even as its power increased. Perhaps, Laura wondered, this was the reason Frank Jordan had decided to leave its anonymous ranks in order to work for Sam.

'Such a merger would mean the end of my father's company,' she said quietly.

'Not necessarily,' Andrew Dillon smiled. 'The name might well remain the same. Your product line might not change appreciably. But Schell would, of course, have management responsibility and control of your Board. You yourself, Miss Christensen, would certainly have a place within your company—or, if you preferred, you could of course live quite well on what the merger would bring you.'

Inwardly Laura felt a rush of anger at the implacable calm of the man before her. She knew that absorption by Schell would destroy the independent company her father had slaved thirty years to build. Many of the executives he had trained so carefully would be fired, and the practices he had begun in product development would be superseded by Schell's own ideas. Christensen Products would be no more than a paper company.

'If you like,' Andrew Dillon was saying, 'I can look into the situation myself. A little informal chat with Roy Schell could do no harm. I can simply mention that you might be interested in a merger—at the right price, of course, and on the right terms.'

Laura took a deep breath.

'Let me discuss this with my own people,' she sighed, 'and I'll get back to you.'

A frown replaced Andrew Dillon's mild expression.

'Fine,' he said coolly, rising to usher Laura out. 'Let me know what you think. But remember that time is short. If you want to avoid simple bankruptcy we'll have to move with alacrity. One has to prepare the ground for these things. And one more thing, Miss Christensen: please accept my sympathy over Sam's tragic death.'

'Thank you, Mr Dillon. I'll be in touch.'

'I'm afraid First Federal is right about one thing, Laura. Sam left the company in a dangerously overextended condition, and we're going to have to do something about it.'

Fearfully Laura looked into the tawny irises fixed upon her. Rob Colwell was seated by her side in the conference room adjacent to Sam Christensen's empty office.

'But closing our factories and laying off our workers,' Laura sighed, 'strikes me as hardly more acceptable than bankruptcy.'

'Don't lose your sense of perspective,' Rob warned. 'We're only talking about three factories. Christensen Products will survive this cutback and come back strong when the economy improves. Remember that, Laura. We're down, but we're a long way from out.'

With an effort Laura returned his smile. Nothing could shake Rob's blunt gallantry. Throughout Sam's funeral on Sunday he had remained at her side,

steadfast and silent while several of Sam's distinguished business colleagues, partners and competitors
alike, delivered impassioned eulogies for their lost
friend. And now that Sam's passing had been reported
and his thirty-year stewardship of his beloved
company chronicled in all the business newspapers,
Rob remained as Laura's closest link to Sam himself.

Ten years ago Sam had hired Rob as a fresh-faced
business school graduate bent on making his fortune.
But Rob had soon surprised himself as well as his
employer by showing complete indifference to formal
advancement within the company's ranks. Business, it
turned out, was an entirely intellectual challenge to
him. He cared only to understand the corporation in
its most intimate workings, and to offer a consultant's
advice on the best strategies for improving its sales
and productivity.

And, above all, he cared for Sam Christensen. For
years he had been Sam's executive assistant and
troubleshooter, and no Christensen executive dared
claim either Rob's encyclopaedic knowledge of the
company's far-flung operations or his privileged
status in the eyes of its founder.

The two men's nocturnal telephone conversations
had become the object of wry speculation on the part
of the other executives. Rob's phone would ring at
three or four in the morning, and he would rub the
sleep out of his eyes as Sam's ruminative voice filled
his ear.

'Rob,' Sam would say, 'I've been looking at our
Florida sales and thinking about what you said this
morning.'

In Rob's benumbed state the previous morning
seemed light years from the present. He had to struggle
to recall what his insomniac boss was talking about.

'Now, if that market is going sour because of the oil
shortage,' the disembodied voice went on, 'the

conventional wisdom would suggest that we cut our advertising budget down south and pull in our belts for a while. Am I making sense?'

'Well, sir, it depends . . .'

'My thoughts exactly, Rob. My thoughts exactly. Perhaps the conventional wisdom is wrong this time. Suppose Christensen were to hit that market for all it's worth, now that everyone else is unsure of what to do. We're strong enough in New England to absorb a bit of a loss . . .'

'Then,' Rob yawned, 'when the tide turns . . .'

'Exactly,' Sam laughed. 'We'll be stronger than ever in small industry. Let's talk about this tomorrow early, Rob. And Rob?'

'Yes, sir?'

'I'm just looking at the time. Awfully sorry if I woke you up.'

'Don't mention it, Sam.'

Thus a new idea would be born through Christensen Products' nocturnal hot line. As he brooded in his bathrobe over the reports and projections on his desk at home, Sam would reach reflexively for his telephone and dial Rob's number without a glance at the clock or a conscious notion of what he planned to say. But the sound of his trusted confidant's voice sufficed to unleash a stream of thoughts which often contained the key to the company's future.

Sam Christensen adored Rob Colwell for his loyalty and intellect. For Laura, then in her teens, her father's handsome young assistant had another sort of aura. With his strong, athletic frame and curly hair tinged with a fugitive hint of red, Rob was the image of youthful vitality and virile charm. Since he came to dinner often at the Everit Street house, Laura had more than her share of opportunities to cast diffident glances of admiration at him, and to blush with embarrassment when he smiled acknowledgment.

In those days Laura had not yet grown into the confident and creative young woman who was to emerge from her college years. She was a pretty teenager whose laughing eyes and blossoming figure concealed a personality which still had rough edges. Though Rob might well have noticed the painfully romantic longings which tied her tongue in his presence, his attitude was anything but condescending. Whenever the intensity of his conversations with Sam allowed a few moments' breathing space, Rob drew Laura out on her plans for the future. He encouraged her interest in engineering, speaking knowledgeably on the subject himself.

To make matters yet more thrilling, Rob always noticed Laura's clothes and hair. His relaxed compliments, proferred in private so as not to draw attention to her in front of Sam, only served to increase his prestige in her imagination, for she attributed to them the same incontrovertible authority that Sam found in his invaluable advice.

Though the torch Laura carried for Rob Colwell dimmed as her adolescence gave way to college life and new ambitions, it left its mark upon her. The memory of Rob's quiet confidence and daunting male attractiveness hung at the back of her mind, and in comparison with it the excitable young men she met at school seemed oddly shallow. She found herself immersed in her academic work without second thoughts about the relative lack of romance in her life, inwardly confident that when the time was right a man of Rob's mature virility would cross her path.

When she returned to Christensen as an employee she became fully aware of Rob's enormous importance to the company, and felt a twinge of involuntary trepidation in his presence. He seemed even more handsome than four years before, for the passage of time had sharpened his incisive, self-assured demeanour. A supremely eligible young professional, he was possessed of a business acumen which was more than a little intimidating.

To Laura's immense relief he welcomed her to the company with open arms, and made a point of visiting her small office at regular intervals for encouraging conversations. The four years that followed saw the blossoming of their friendship as well as their professional relationship. As Laura's own responsibilities within the corporation increased, Rob offered constant advice and moral support. The buoying caress of his smiling eyes became a virtual extension of the aura of happy camaraderie which emanated from Sam Christensen's irrepressible personality.

But today Rob's expression was hooded by concern, and his jaw set in deep concentration on the urgent business at hand.

'Zalman, I think you agree on which facilities will have to go.' Rob turned to Zalman Corey, Christensen's Vice-President in charge of Finance, who adjusted his horn-rimmed glasses nervously as he removed a sheet of paper from his briefcase.

'I'll tell you what I told Sam before his death,' Zalman said quickly. 'Our weakest points are Springfield, Albany and Rochester. If we close plants in those three places, sell the properties and eliminate the payroll, the financial benefit will probably see us through. Some of our product lines will, of course, have to be eliminated . . .'

'When you say "probably",' Laura interjected, 'do you mean that bankruptcy is still a possibility?'

Zalman Corey pulled at his tie. 'Only if things get a hell of a lot worse across the board in the next two quarters,' he said. 'Pardon my language,' he added sheepishly.

Laura turned to Rob. 'And you concur in this?' she asked.

'I think Zalman has said what needs to be said,' Rob nodded. 'Sam built Christensen into a very secure corporation, Laura. I wouldn't want you to think he in any way mismanaged the company. But he expanded our facilities during a more secure period. The point is that no one is safe nowadays.'

Laura frowned in consternation. She had hopefully conjectured that Andrew Dillon's alarming words were merely calculated to achieve some sort of psychological advantage over her. But now her most trusted colleagues seemed to suggest that Sam had left his company in a state of grave peril indeed.

'One more thing,' she said, intentionally keeping silent about Andrew Dillon's mention of Schell International. 'What about a merger?'

Rob shook his head. 'That's always a possibility for a company the size of Christensen, whose products have a good reputation. But in today's market the terms of a merger would not be favourable to us. No one will want to pay us what we're worth.'

Zalman Corey nodded ruminatively.

'However,' Laura pursued, 'if whatever cutbacks we make don't solve our problems, we might be forced to accept absorption by some national or multinational corporation somewhere down the line—and on even worse terms than we would get today.'

'Anything is possible, Laura.' Rob Colwell's eyes were grim. 'The worst eventuality as well as the best.'

'What I don't understand,' Laura said, 'is how we can be faced with such a choice so soon after Dad's death. I have the feeling that the whole picture has changed simply because he's been ... eliminated from it.'

'I don't think Sam wanted to worry you with all this before his untimely passing, Laura,' Zalman Corey said. 'He knew there were hard times coming, but he was, or considered himself to be, in the prime of health. Sam was a brave man, and a very bright one.

He simply assumed he would get us through this with a minimum of damage to the company.'

And perhaps he would have, Laura thought with a pang of grief for Christensen's lost leader. If Sam saw fit to run his company on a business-as-usual basis in the face of financial pressure from First Federal Bank, it could only have been because he had reason to believe his wit and guile would allow him to prevail. But the plans he had in his mind had followed him to the grave.

'Frank, you haven't said anything.' Rob turned to glance across the conference table's rich walnut expanse. As she followed his gaze to the chair in which Frank Jordan had sat in silence since the conversation began, Laura realised that a fearful instinct had made her avoid looking in his direction until now. In her own mind Frank still bore the sign of the monstrous Schell conglomerate whose power Andrew Dillon had evoked so blandly. She wondered whether the urgency of Christensen Products' predicament struck him as a novel experience after his years with the indestructible Schell empire.

Through his black eyes Frank made an inscrutable gesture which was neither agreement nor disagreement. But Laura could feel the quick turning of the wheels in his analytical mind.

'Well,' Rob turned back to her with a trace of discomfort, 'we'll all think it over. But there's one more important piece of business that has to be mentioned before we break up. I've been on the phone with some of our Board members, Laura, and we've found a curious amendment to our bylaws that Sam pushed through not long ago. According to this amendment, in the event of the company president's sudden death or departure, the majority stockholder becomes chief executive officer until such time as a new president is named.'

'I don't understand,' Laura said. In the hectic days since Sam's death she had not found time to dwell on Christensen's executive hierarchy, and had simply assumed that a new president would eventually be chosen by the Board from among the officers Sam had respected most.

'Well,' Rob smiled, 'since Sam left all his stock to you, Laura, you are now the majority stockholder. That means you are now President of Christensen Products.'

The shock occasioned by his words left Laura numb. She heard none of the casual remarks exchanged by her colleagues as they drifted from the room. But in a corner of her field of vision she thought she saw a slight smile curl Frank Jordan's tight lips.

It was a smile of amusement and of contempt.

CHAPTER THREE

SCHELL, ARMAND, *mfr.; born Prague, Sept. 11, 1900; son of Janek and Sofia Schell; emigrated 1916; American citizenship 1921; B.S., Columbia University,* Summa cum laude, *1919. With American Can Co., Forest Park, N.J. 1919–20. Successively member field sales staff, asst. district sales mgr., vice pres. sales. 1922 founded New Jersey Metal. Expansion throughout East Coast (incl. acquisition of American Can) 1920s. 1930 company name changed to Schell Inc. 1930s expansion incl. electronics, communications, construction, shipbuilding subsidiaries. 1937 company name changed to Schell International Inc., multi-national corp. with subsidiaries throughout W. Europe, S. America. 1940–5 weapons and ship mfr. for Allies; acquisitions incl. insurance companies, banks, hotels. 1940s advisor to Presidents Roosevelt, Truman. 1950 pres., NYC Fiscal Action Board. 1952 Special Envoy, European Financial Congress. President, Board chmn. Schell International Inc. 1937– Company assets as of 1979: $33 billion.*

Mar. Andrea V. Morgan, June 19, 1928. Children: Anton Schell, b. 1932 (q.v.), Roy Schell, b. 1938 (q.v.). Second marriage to Barbara Bond (cf. Andrew Bond, 1911–), Oct. 6, 1952. Divorced 1970. Daughter, Julia Bond Schell, b. 1958.

An endless list of fellowships, memberships and honorary degrees followed, filling an entire page of the volume of *Who's Who in Finance and Industry* which lay open on the desk before Laura. With a sigh she turned her tired eyes from the columns of fine print and considered the story of ruthless ambition hidden between their lines.

When still in his teens Armand Schell had completed his college education and begun a business career that straddled wars, depressions and recessions without a single false step. Turning world events unfailingly to his own advantage, he had risen to a pinnacle of political and financial influence unmatched by any single business figure since Rockefeller.

But the clipped biography made no reference to what was common knowledge in the business community. Armand Schell, a legend in his own time, was past his prime and in failing health. His two sons controlled the inner workings of Schell International and made most of its decisions on acquisitions. Most observers had concluded that with advancing age the conglomerate's founder had either lost interest in what he once termed his 'mission' as a manufacturer, or was simply too weak to resist the new generation of profit-oriented executives headed by his sons. As a result, Schell International was rapidly becoming a crazy quilt of unrelated companies whose interests often conflicted with one another. Yet its profits continued to grow apace, for dozens of governments around the world were beholden to Schell for important investments.

No longer a corporate innovator, Schell was now an essentially financial institution whose sheer dimensions defied precise description. Few sovereign nations could match its gross yearly product.

It was the last corporation in the world one would choose for an enemy.

Roy Schell and his brother Anton had their own short entries in *Who's Who*. Of Julia Bond Schell, the young daughter of Armand's unsuccessful second marriage, little was known. It was rumoured that the girl—whose delicate beauty shone forth from the rare news photos depicting her attendance at social and cultural events—lacked all interest in her father's business empire, and avoided the limelight intentionally.

Leaving the book open before her, Laura stared exhaustedly into space. The office was in darkness save for the fluorescent desk lamp whose beam illuminated the heavy volume. The digital clock beside the pen set Laura had given Sam six years ago read 11:36 p.m. Its large numbers, a balm for Sam's weak eyes, glowed emerald green against the obscurity behind.

No sound came from the corridor beyond the secretaries' empty office. Ernst, the elderly watchman with whom Sam had occasionally gone fishing on Sundays in summer, would be on a lower floor at this hour, mopping and dusting and emptying waste baskets with unhurried movements as he shook his head in disapproval of the fate that had torn his friend and boss from him.

Sam's huge desk was an unfamiliar landscape in the penumbra. Beside its old-fashioned blotter were Laura's graduation picture and an old portrait photo of her mother. The snapshot of Sam with his prize bass, taken by Laura on a carefree vacation in Maine, was a grey shadow on a distant wall. Surrounding it were framed pictures of Sam shaking hands with government officials, corporation presidents and friends. On another wall a profusion of testimonials and honorary diplomas reflected the pale light of the desk lamp.

As a child Laura had considered these accoutrements of a proud career as familiar furnishings, domestic and friendly. They were the cheerful background against which her laughing father took her on his knee, whirled her playfully in his huge swivel chair, and showed her off to his executives and secretaries.

Only when she came to work for Sam had she realised that those pictures and diplomas testified to the full significance of his enormous achievements in business, and to the shrewdness and dedication with which he had built Christensen into an internationally respected corporation.

Now the walls, the smiling faces in their fragile frames, and even the lifeless pens in their marble stand had a bleak air of supplication. The spirit that had animated this office was gone forever. No one could bring it back.

And before long this office might not even exist in its present form. A new occupant and new, foreign furnishings might appear to wipe away the memory of Sam Christensen's sunlit life—unless something was done now to protect his legacy.

Why did you have to die? Laura thought miserably, a sudden upsurge of grief bringing tears to her eyes.

The contradiction of death seemed unbearably immediate. Sam was gone forever, and yet the cheerful rumble of his confident voice still echoed in all the corners of the room. Laura could almost feel his protective warmth enfolding her in the shadows, for the comfortable executive chair, tailored to his portly dimensions, was deliciously restful. Were it not for the crisis that had driven her here she might have lapsed into childlike slumber in its vast leather expanse.

She should be home in bed, she told herself irritably. Fatigue was tearing dangerously at her emotions. And heaven knew she would need her sleep.

But the revelations of the day had left her nerves on edge. She had come to Sam's office as President of his company, determined to get a feel for her new responsibility. Yet here she sat, paralysed by the irony of her situation. Sam had his wish: Laura had inherited his power and his position. But only his tragic and untimely death had made his dream come true, and his bereft daughter was far from capable of handling the job.

On the shelf behind her lay the financial reports on Christensen's plants in Rochester, Springfield and Albany. Their bland columns of figures told precisely the story Zalman Corey had outlined this afternoon. The three factories were running at half capacity, and since Sam had laid off as few workers as possible, they were generating huge losses. Rob had written them off bluntly.

Zalman, I think you agree on which facilities will have to go.

As a girl Laura had accompanied her father on visits to those branches. She had seen faces light up as Sam hurried along the assembly lines, shaking hands, joking with workers whose names he unfailingly remembered, accepting the friendly barbs directed at him, and enquiring about the health problems and academic successes of his employees' children. Everyone seemed to smile upon him with familial tenderness as they exclaimed over the extent of Laura's growth since her last visit.

Our weakest points are Springfield, Albany and Rochester. If we close plants in those three places, the financial benefit will probably see us through.

Now Laura was expected to lay off all those loyal, hard-working people. She could imagine their unsuccessful job searches in this day of high unemployment, and the long hours they would spend doing crossword puzzles or reading paperback books in the state unemployment offices while styrofoam cups of coffee cooled in their hands. The men in middle age would not find jobs to replace those they had lost at Christensen. Their pensions would be lost. In all likelihood the effects of their joblessness would quickly extend to the education of the very children whose names Sam used to recall so casually.

And when it was all over those idle workers would sigh philosophically and trace the origin of their misfortune to Sam's death and his daughter's accession to control of the corporation.

Some of our product lines will, of course, have to be eliminated . . .

Alone in the quiet office, Laura shook her head.

'Something about this isn't right,' she thought, pursing her lips in frustration. Andrew Dillon's ultimatum, so shockingly absolute in the wake of Sam's sudden death, had an odd ring, as did Zalman Corey's seemingly ready-made suggestion to reduce overheads by closing factories. And there was the crucial fact that Sam himself had made no provision at all for such a move.

Sam must have known something important which allowed him to conclude that production cutbacks would not be necessary, despite his company's financial woes.

But what? What did he know?

'I have to find out,' Laura thought grimly, rebelling at the notion of being browbeaten into submission. Everyone seemed convinced that her inexperience required her to accept this blow to Christensen Products with suitable meekness. Only the shade of Sam's indefatigable spirit urged her silently to refuse to give in.

'They won't have me that cheap,' she murmured to herself in stubborn defiance. If she lacked the expertise to see a clear solution to her dilemma, she at least possessed the will to find it at all costs.

'Head spinning?'

With a start she looked up, frightened by the deep voice that had torn her from her reverie. Frank Jordan stood before her in the half-light, his jacket thrown over his shoulder, his open collar revealing the dark web of curly hair covering his deep chest.

She frowned, irked to see him loom so close to her when she had thought she was alone.

'I didn't hear you come in,' she said coolly.

'I knocked at the door,' he smiled. 'You seemed lost in thought.'

She had to look up into the blackness beyond the lampshade to see the face above his long limbs. A hint of mockery quirked his dark brow as he gazed down at her.

'What brings you here at this hour?' she asked, straightening a lock of her tangled hair.

'I was on my way out,' he said, 'and stopped by because something told me you might be here. I can see you're your father's daughter. Burning the midnight oil, just like Sam.'

She could think of no response, for the arrogance of his tone made it plain that he found her efforts at leadership amusing. She recalled the snide look in his eyes after Rob dropped his bombshell about her new position.

Having noticed the open book before her, Frank placed his large hands on the desk top and leaned closer to her. His clean male scent seemed to cover her suddenly, and she could feel the warmth of his breath. Reflecting that she had never found herself at such close quarters with him before, Laura had to force herself to meet the penetrating eyes fixed on her.

'Dillon mentioned Schell International to you, didn't he?' he asked abruptly.

'I beg your pardon?' she returned.

'Andrew Dillon,' he said. 'He talked about possible mergers when you went to see him, didn't he? That's why you were asking about the idea today, wasn't it? And he mentioned Schell, didn't he?'

Unnerved by his stabbing questions, Laura struggled to control her anger.

'What gives you that idea?' she asked curtly. 'And

what difference does it make? You heard what Rob
said.'

He leaned closer to her, the hard lines of his tanned
face adding their force to his sharp words.

'It isn't hard to put two and two together,' he said.
'You're sitting here in the middle of the night poring
over *Who's Who*. I can read upside down, Miss
Christensen. It's a talent that's easy to develop. Now,
what could make you so interested in Armand Schell?
Someone must have drawn your attention to his
corporation.'

'All right,' Laura sighed irritably. 'Yes, his name
was mentioned. What of it?'

'And I did hear what Rob Colwell said,' he added.
'He said a merger would be disadvantageous to
Christensen. That, by the way, was the only
competent piece of advice you were given today.'

He sat down in the chair opposite Laura, his eyes
appraising her reaction to his words.

'I'm sure I don't know what you're talking about,'
she said, bristling at his arrogance.

'I can see that,' he agreed ironically. 'You have quite
a problem, Miss Christensen. Your company is about
to go down the drain, and you don't know what any of
it is all about. Do you?'

Appalled by his condescension, Laura felt a rush of
anger in her tired nerves.

'If you came up here to insult me . . .' she began.

'Not to insult you,' he cut her off. 'To warn you.
And, if possible, to talk some sense into you. You're
going to need all of it you can find, and in a hurry.'

Laura regarded him in silence for a long moment,
determined not to allow his imperious demeanour to
cow her. This day had been bad enough already
without his invasion of her privacy. Yet something in
his intense gaze dissuaded her from simply asking him
to leave.

'Do you intend to explain yourself?' she asked at last.

'I'm going to try,' he said calmly. 'But it won't be easy, because you're not experienced enough to understand what is at stake in all this. I respected your father, Miss Christensen, but I think he made a silly mistake in setting things up so that you'd inherit a responsibility so far over your head. He loved this company, but in his ambition for you he may have destroyed it.'

Stung by his words, Laura would have loved to send him away with a comment to match his own insolence. Yet his accusation was not without its grain of painful truth. With an effort of will she resolved to find out what was in his mind.

'Leaving aside my incompetence to evaluate what you came here to say,' she said, 'why don't you just come out with it, Mr Jordan?'

'All right,' he responded without taking his eyes from her. 'Your friend Colwell and Zalman Corey have given you some bad advice. If you follow it, you'll be playing right into Andrew Dillon's hands. And don't believe he's bluffing. He's in earnest.'

'Why do you say that?' Laura asked.

'Because I know him. I know his type.' Frank's eyes narrowed. 'Dillon is expecting you to run scared by reducing overhead and cutting back production. That will weaken your company enough for him to flatten it when the short-term debt comes due—or before, if it suits him. He's gambling that your fear will blind you to the reality. And his gamble seems to be paying off.'

'I don't see . . .' Laura stammered.

'No, you don't,' he interrupted. 'That's obvious. But Sam saw, didn't he, Miss Christensen? Sam knew there was no reason to fear First Federal in the short run. That's why he had no intention of closing factories or dropping product lines. But now Sam is gone, isn't he?'

Carefully Laura scrutinised the firm lines of his handsome face. His gaze was pitiless, unforgiving. The careless waves of his black hair lent a roguish grace to his athletic form as he sat before her. His impertinence was unbearable, but the truth of his words was too penetrating to deny. In a trice he had probed to the essence of Laura's dilemma.

'As I see it,' he went on, 'your advisers have been living in too small a pond. They don't understand how corporate takeovers happen.'

'And I suppose you do,' Laura shot back.

'I've had some experience in the area,' he nodded, impervious to her sarcasm. 'I know Dillon, and I know Schell International. I also know something you haven't bothered to find out, and would probably never know if I weren't here to tell you: how the two are connected.'

'Connected?' Laura asked, taken aback. 'How?'

'Let me explain something to you,' he said, his hands motionless on the arms of his chair. 'A banker is not an impersonal institution, shrouded in old walnut and fancy board rooms, the way they like to pretend. A banker is an investor, no different from any speculator on the market. He puts his money into a lot of stocks, some more dependable than others. He can make mistakes, get in over his head, and lose money, just as you or I would.'

He paused, his dark eyes resting implacably upon her.

'Now, Andrew Dillon is in over his head right now,' he went on. 'First Federal's portfolio has been losing money for some years now. So Dillon is hanging on to the coat-tails of a man named Roy Schell. He's put every dollar he can find into a holding company called Beta Concepts, of which Roy Schell is the brains and major stockholder. The future of First Federal depends on that arrangement. Now, are you beginning to smell a conflict of interest?'

Laura frowned. 'You mean,' she said, 'that Dillon is beholden to Schell.'

'More than beholden,' he said. 'He practically works for Roy. He acts for Beta Concepts. Has to, in fact. That's where his money is, and where his tips come from. He's not the first banker to fall in with a conglomerator like Roy Schell, and he won't be the last. Now, you can't expect a fellow like him to consider the best interests of a modest operation like Christensen when he has millions tied up in something so much bigger. Can you?'

'But where is the conflict of interest?' Laura asked.

'There wasn't any,' he said with a wry smile, 'until Dillon mentioned Schell International to you. That's when he gave himself away. If you knew Dillon, you'd know that his very mention of a merger with Schell proves that Roy had already told him he wanted to absorb Christensen. That's the only explanation possible.'

If Laura's head had not been spinning before, it certainly was now. Frank's revelations were as confusing as they were sinister.

'What makes you so sure of all this?' she asked.

'I wasn't at first,' he shrugged. 'It was a pretty solid hunch. But I haven't been working late today myself simply in order to impress my new boss, Miss Christensen. I've been doing a little checking, and I found out something that will interest you. Only hours after Andrew Dillon threatened you with bankruptcy, his bank was buying 50,000 shares of Christensen Products stock. It certainly looks as though he has more confidence in this company than he led you to believe, doesn't it?'

Laura shook her head in bewilderment. 'I don't understand,' she said.

'And not long afterwards,' he went on, 'a mutual fund called Barns & Porter, whose president is a close friend of Roy Schell, bought 65,000 shares of Christensen. For three days now there has been unusual movement in Christensen shares. Too much movement. Understandably, some of your long-time shareholders are nervous in the wake of Sam's death. So they're selling. But what is interesting is who is buying, and in such large amounts.'

'What does it mean?' Laura asked, hopelessly over her head in the welter of information he was forcing upon her.

'It means, young lady, that the raiders are upon you. Roy Schell is an expert at acquiring companies. He is quietly buying into your stock—using cover names to conceal himself—and influencing other speculators to do the same. These people all owe him favours, so when he tells them to buy or sell a stock, they obey. When he feels the time is right, he'll make a tender offer to all your stockholders at so attractive a price that they'll sell. Then he'll have enough of his people on your Board to force you to give up the company.'

'I'm sorry,' Laura sighed, 'but what is a tender offer?'

He shook his head in ill-concealed amazement at her ignorance. 'Let's suppose that Roy Schell has accumulated around 10 per cent of your company's stock,' he said. 'Now, he makes a public tender offer, either through full-page ads in the business papers or through direct mailings to your stockholders. He offers them either cash or equivalent stock in one of his own companies—say, Beta Concepts. The exchange rate he proposes is something they can't refuse, such as $1.75 or even $2.00 for every dollar of Christensen stock they own. Since they're seduced by the quick profit to be made on the deal, they sell. And, of course, his personal friends like Andrew Dillon will sell when he tells them to. The result is that overnight Roy has taken over a huge block of your stock.'

'But doesn't he lose an awful lot of money by paying double for our shares?' Laura asked.

'His loss is tax deductible,' Frank smiled. 'That's just one of the loopholes that allows this sort of thing to happen in business today.'

Passing a tired hand over her furrowed brow, Laura fought to concentrate on the import of his words.

'But what about me?' she asked at last. 'I'm the majority stockholder. He can't make me sell *my* shares.'

'Good point,' Frank said. 'But he's thought of that, too. He's gambling that the short-term debt pressure you're under will force you to cut back production. Thus your price-earnings ratio will go down, and your stock will lose its value. Christensen Products will have a weak profile on the market. Then, of course, your shareholders will be all the more eager to sell. After Roy has accumulated enough shares for himself, he'll lower the boom by staging nasty proxy fight in which you'll be accused of mismanaging the company since Sam's death, and of being the incompetent one-woman majority stockholder who's ruining the company through her stubbornness. At that point you'll own 51 per cent of nothing, Miss Christensen, and you'll be humiliated into selling out simply in order to save your employees' jobs. That's how the game is played. I've seen it many times.'

He shrugged indifferently. 'Of course,' he added, 'their jobs won't be safe. Roy will fire all your top executives and replace them with people who take orders from him. Christensen Products, as Sam knew it, will cease to exist. The company will be nothing more than a piece of paper in Roy Schell's portfolio.'

Horrified by the picture he had painted of her corporation's future, Laura gazed in dismay at his reclining form.

'But why?' she asked, unable to suppress the

beseeching tone in her voice. 'Why is Christensen so important to him? Why us?'

'For investment purposes,' he responded blandly. 'Roy is a speculator. He deals in the hundreds of millions of dollars every month. He lives by manipulating stock prices, buying and selling companies, and taking losses for tax purposes while reaping profits on the Exchange. It's all a game to him—but a deadly one. He probably had his eye on Christensen long ago, but he must have known that Sam was too clever a man to let the company be taken over. Then, when Sam died and a crazy bylaw left Christensen without leadership, Roy saw his chance to move in for the kill. He called Andrew Dillon and a few other friends—and here you are, Miss Christensen, green as a calf, the ideal victim.'

'I suppose this is all a game to you, too,' Laura returned bleakly, hurt by his pitiless words.

'If you like,' he said coldly. 'I've been around people like Roy long enough to know the score.'

'Why have you bothered to tell me all this,' Laura asked bitterly, 'if there is no hope?'

'I didn't say there was no hope,' he said. 'There are ways to win a fight like this—if you have enough experience, and are smart enough to take some calculated risks.'

'Which I'm not,' Laura said. 'According to you, that is.'

'Time will tell,' he replied, raising an eyebrow speculatively as he held her with his stare. 'You're Sam's daughter. Sam was a smart man. You may be in over your head at the moment, but it's not impossible to rise above oneself if the situation requires it. In the meantime, Miss Christensen, you're not alone.'

'What do you mean?'

'I'm here to help you, if I can,' he said. 'I came to work for Sam because I admired the company he had built. Now he's gone, and through his own ill-advised plans for you he has put his life's work in jeopardy. But if you can be made to behave like an honest-to-God executive—which, as you say, you're not—we'll have a slim chance of forcing Schell to back off.'

'Wouldn't you feel more comfortable doing the job yourself?' Laura asked sharply. 'I'm sure the burden of my incompetence can't help the company.'

'You said it, I didn't.' His smile was sardonic. 'But to answer your question, I have no interest in a company presidency for myself. Not at the moment, anyway. I came here to help Sam—not to take over. His death hasn't changed that.'

Infuriated by his complacency, Laura would have loved to find words to bring him up short. But the very axis of her existence had been hopelessly skewed by his frightening news, and suddenly it seemed that his shrewd intellect was the only ally that might save her from disaster. As she contemplated the straight contours of his powerful man's body, cursing the fate that had so suddenly made her dependent upon him, she resolved to swallow her pride and benefit as much as possible from his obvious expertise.

'All right,' she said at last. 'What do you suggest?'

He crossed his arms calmly. 'Dillon and Schell are counting on your inexperience and that of your advisers in defending yourself against a takeover,' he said. 'They're expecting you to react in fear to what happens. They correctly assume that if you drop assets and cut production, Christensen will be further weakened. The short-term debt is their main weapon. Therefore there is only one realistic way to defeat them.'

'What?' Laura asked.

'Don't react to what they do. Act, Miss Christensen. Make *them* react to *you*.'

His regard was inscrutable as Laura weighed his words.

'I don't understand,' she said hesitantly.

'They want you to make cutbacks. Therefore you expand. You produce. They want you to run scared. Therefore you act boldly. And most importantly, since they want you to behave as an impoverished corporation, the answer is simple: behave like the healthy and strong company Christensen really is. Make profit. Make the price of your stock go up, so that your own shareholders will be reluctant to sell. Make them understand that a merger will not be in their own best interest. If you do those things, Roy Schell will shrug his shoulders and look for a more pliant victim. He'll discourage easily when he sees that you're tougher than he thought.'

'But isn't that rather a tall order?' Laura asked in perplexity. 'You heard Zalman and Rob today . . .'

'It may be a tall order,' he said, 'but it's the only way. Either you make yourself some solid short-term profit and pay off those First Federal notes, or you're finished. It's as simple as that.'

He must have sensed her helplessness, for he went on in a gentler tone.

'I've seen it done before, Laura. A lot of companies have made fortunes overnight by keeping a sharp eye on the marketplace. It takes imagination and initiative, and a solid production base. You already have the base; Sam saw to that. All you have to do is use it for all it's worth. Look for the short-term profit Sam was too conservative to go after. Be aggressive. Take risks. It's your only chance, but it's worth a try.'

A quiet laugh escaped his lips as he leaned forward. 'I'm sorry,' he said. 'May I call you Laura? Or would you prefer Boss?'

Ignoring his irony, she pondered the logic of his recommendation. Though it seemed daring and even reckless on the surface, it might indeed prove necessary if the information he had brought her was correct. She would verify his claims about Andrew Dillon on her own. But to implement his advice was another matter entirely.

'And where is this short-term profit supposed to come from?' she asked.

'You'll find out,' he said. 'You've been here a lot longer than I have, and you've lived a lifetime with Sam. You know the company's basic strengths. Examine them. Go through your inventory and research analyses with a fine-toothed comb. Consult your advisers. Pick their brains. Talk to your sales staff. Look for that soft spot where the market will respond to a good, hard campaign. This corporation is a machine designed to turn production into profit. Make it work, Laura.'

He had stood up, and towered above her once more in the darkened office.

'But don't take too long,' he concluded. 'Time is short for you, and Roy Schell knows it.'

'You ask a lot,' she said, her tired eyes straying over the taut lines of his face and body. Clearly he was all dauntless strength and confidence, from his muscular limbs to his incisive mind. A perfect stranger to the fear that had coiled itself around Laura, he expected her to behave as he would in her situation.

'It's the job that asks a lot,' he corrected her. 'If you have to rise above yourself in order to fill it, then do it. I think I knew Sam well enough to know that that would have been his opinion.'

He glanced at the framed pictures on the far wall.

'Your dad was quite a man,' he said. 'He must have had a lot of faith in you, Laura, since he got you into this fix. You might as well give it your best effort, win or lose.'

His lips curled into a smile of amused sympathy as he looked down at her.

'But you can't go about the business of saving your

company until you've had a good night's sleep,' he
said. 'It's time you were in bed. Shall I walk you
downstairs?'

Her fatigue dulling her senses, Laura stood up with
a sigh. He had taken her coat from its hanger and was
holding it for her. As she slipped her arms into the
sleeves she felt the warmth of his large hands on her
shoulders. The urgent power of his man's will was
palpable even in the momentary caress of his palms,
and for an insidious instant Laura felt a shudder of
yielding steal down her back and through her
exhausted limbs.

She fumbled in her purse for the office key,
unnerved by the sexual ember that lurked behind
Frank Jordan's incisive personality. He was the sort of
man, she mused, who would offer encouragement only
as a prelude to further demands. A man whose
sympathy was in the service of his iron determination
to have things his way.

And even now, as he held the outer door open for
her with a smile, he seemed to have her in his power.
Rebelling instinctively against her own vulnerability,
she thought of the world of ruthless intrigue from
which he had emerged when he came to work for Sam
only a month ago. Now that unseen world had wound
its tentacles around her own future in a cruel grip.
Frank Jordan had offered to lead her through it to
safety, because he knew its dangers and its challenges.
But did this not mean that he was still at home in the
heartless exterior which threatened her, and still
belonged to it?

She hated to allow herself to be led by a stranger.
Yet she had no choice.

Or was it Frank himself who made it seem that there
was no choice? She could not tell, but she intended to
find out.

They stood side by side in silence as the elevator

rushed downward. The doors opened to reveal the empty lobby. A security guard sat quietly at his desk, viewing a bank of closed-circuit television screens which must have chronicled their descent from Sam's office. Laura greeted him with a forced smile as she passed.

The night wind blew her hair wildly against her collar as Frank held the door for her.

'Mr Jordan . . .' she began as she prepared to hurry home to bed.

'Frank,' he corrected, extending a long finger to arrange the silken strands of hair.

'Frank,' she said, struck by the novel sound of the name on her lips. 'I appreciate your . . .'

'Think nothing of it, Laura. I'm sorry if I was rough on you upstairs. Under the circumstances, it seemed necessary. Do you need a lift?'

'No, thanks. My car is right here.'

'Goodnight, then.'

He took his leave of her with an easy smile. But as she watched him recede into the darkness, the invisible depths of his own mind seemed as impenetrable as the night.

CHAPTER FOUR

THE two weeks that followed Laura's nocturnal encounter with Frank Jordan were the most difficult of her life. Fighting the sinking feeling in her stomach at every instant, she resolved to transform herself almost overnight into the shrewd and experienced woman whose initiative might save Christensen Products from certain disaster.

The process was agonising, for she could not suppress her suspicion that the real Laura Christensen was being lost in the maelstrom of her forced metamorphosis. Behind every deliberate action she took, she heard a stifled murmur of protest from the frightened, grief-stricken girl she remained inside.

Yet oddly enough, she would later recall, the very desperation of her sudden corporate responsibility went a long way towards distracting her from the throes of mourning Sam's death. Though he was gone now, his spirit seemed to summon her to pour her energies into the challenging job he had bequeathed to her. Surveying from his own office the company he had built singlehandedly, she felt comfortingly close to him in her very solitude.

Systematically Laura moved from department to department within Christensen's headquarters, personally scrutinising every important page of the mountain of paperwork in which the company's past and present were described and catalogued. Immersing herself in balance sheets, contracts, payrolls, materials cost estimates and sales figures, she fought to capture for herself some of the intimate knowledge of the company as a living entity that had come so naturally to Sam.

Though the books and records could not predict Christensen's future, Laura began to discover dark corners in which surplus assets had been stored by Sam for just such a rainy day as this. Most were holdings in real estate. Some were blocks of stock held in companies across the country whose solid sales had attracted Sam's interest.

Laura wondered whether these surplus assets had figured in Sam's unspoken plans for safeguarding his corporation in this harsh economy.

She could not tell.

But even as she learned of Christensen's hidden resources, and saw the evidence of its strength and productivity, Laura made herself an unwilling expert on the company's short-term debt and its dangerous consequences. She saw how Sam's expansions had made the firm more healthy and vibrant while unavoidably leaving it vulnerable. It was like a growing child, sound and vigorous, yet still tender as it developed towards its full potential.

Now Laura understood why Christensen was in so sudden a crisis. Its fate was knitted into that of the entire East Coast, and even of the nation. The recession had forced factories to close everywhere— factories whose production lines would have required precision parts supplied by Christensen Products. And as factories had closed, workers had been laid off— workers who would have spent some of their wages on small appliances manufactured by Christensen.

It was a vicious circle. And there was no way to escape it until the economy improved. On that point, Rob Colwell and Zalman Corey were undoubtedly right.

Their mistake was to underestimate the true urgency of the situation. As Laura familiarised herself with the subtleties of cash flow, penalty interest rates and undercapitalisation, she realised that Andrew

Dillon had had more than enough ammunition for his threat. There was no guarantee that First Federal's short-term notes could be paid on time without crippling Christensen as a competitive manufacturer.

As the days passed, every division manager within the company's New Haven headquarters received a visit from Laura. When not on her local rounds she telephoned those in charge of Christensen's subsidiaries and plants across the country. Concealing the urgency of her questions as best she could, Laura gently forced those under her authority to reveal the precise condition of their facilities in terms of profit and productivity.

The facts she gleaned were ambiguous. Most of her colleagues candidly spoke of slack sales while protesting their optimism about the future. Laura was left to wonder whether the looks of pained sympathy in their friendly eyes referred to Sam's death alone, or to his grieving daughter's painfully inadequate attempt to fill his shoes. If they knew the company as a whole was in imminent danger, they gave no sign of it.

Laura alone bore that burden.

She had already put the Everit Street house up for sale. The memories haunting its empty rooms would be too disturbing for her to cope with. Besides, she had left the house many years ago, and had become used to apartment living.

When she went there to pick up mail, she cast a loving glance at the Bösendorfer piano which had been one of Sam's rare concessions to his considerable personal wealth. For years Sam had spent quiet hours fumbling his way through simple classical pieces at the beautiful instrument. For his sake Laura had sharpened her performances of the Mozart sonatas and Debussy preludes she had learned as a piano student. Even today she could play some of them from memory, for Sam had never tired of hearing them after his long work days.

The piano would be sold with the house. Having already removed her personal memorabilia, Laura decided to keep a framed watercolour by Franz Kline for which her father had paid thousands of dollars during the first years of the artist's growing fame. Claiming that the abstract composition told a hundred stories, Sam loved to point them out one by one with his short finger. Laura could not bear to give the picture up now, for it was permeated with memories of Sam's bright imagination.

It was with virtual relief that she left the house keys with the estate agent and went back to her immersion in the company. There she crossed paths often with Frank Jordan, whose watchful eyes told her wordlessly that he was waiting for her response to the gathering storm which underlay the apparently routine doings which filled her days.

Occasionally she found herself at close quarters with him in an office or conference room. Though his behaviour was polite and even distant, she could not forget the way his powerful male virility had seemed to loom over her the night he had warned her of the menace to Sam's corporation. Even in his cynical effrontery there was a male assurance that fascinated her. Despite herself she felt beguiled by the sheer strength tensed behind his every word and gesture.

Yet she cursed her own susceptibility, for he had made no secret of his condescension towards her. She was determined to show him that she was not the ineffectual corporate novice he thought her to be. At the same time she intended to evaluate and verify each of his claims about Christensen Products' true peril, for she was not sure she trusted him.

So it was that Laura, when her exhausting days at Christensen Headquarters ended, spent her evenings learning the arcana of corporate mergers, and coming to understand how greedy entrepreneurs succeeded in taking over unsuspecting companies through high-pressure *blitzkrieg* tactics. Underneath the confusing vocabulary of fractional warrants, subordinated convertible debentures and cash tender offers which danced before her eyes, Laura saw the blunt reality. Frank had been right. The danger to Christensen Products went beyond the short-term loans brandished so menacingly by Andrew Dillon.

The sinister activity on the Stock Exchange left no doubt that someone intended to accumulate enough Christensen stock to take over management of the company. Whoever it was possessed enormous influence over the bankers and mutual funds in whose names large blocks of Christensen shares were now registered.

For the moment the process was moving with furtive slowness. Who could know when it might suddenly accelerate?

Laura had managed, through her days of frantic self-education, to see past the trees of her company's inner workings to the forest of its true identity. And the picture that emerged confirmed Frank's frightening assessment of the situation. With its solid reputation, its brilliance in product development, and its momentary fiscal weakness and low stock price, Christensen was the ideal takeover victim.

Profit, as Frank had said, was the only sure answer. Laura must find a way to increase profits dramatically, and with them the price of Christensen common stock—and she must do so almost overnight.

On a windy Thursday evening the answer began to take shape in her mind.

It was nearly midnight. Once again she was alone in Sam's dark office, the silence of the building around her contributing to the concentration she felt she needed. During the last two weeks she had learned to suspend her judgment of the company's long-term fate as she dealt with each day's immediate problems. At night she liked to ruminate in solitude about what her work had taught her.

In less than a week the Board would meet to vote on her accession to the presidency. The result was a foregone conclusion. It amounted to a vote of confidence more than a serious debate. But Laura intended to merit real confidence, come what may.

She had spent the last week pouring determinedly through her Research Division's files. At least two dozen new products were at the prototype stage. No one knew better than Laura that the vast majority of these were small machine parts destined for sale to industry. Their hurried manufacture could scarcely increase profits within the next two quarters, with so many domestic factories closed down or running at half capacity.

Laura's only hope lay with consumer products. If Christensen could reach the public with an affordable and efficient household item within a matter of months—and if profits rose quickly in response to the campaign—the company's peril could be lessened and perhaps eliminated.

But the product must be more than attractive in itself. It must be well suited to working families in the depressed economy of the day. Families with two breadwinners, with children in day-care centres ... households without a lot of money to spare.

On Sam's desk lay design sketches for the dust filtration system her department had worked so hard on over the past year. She had half-persuaded Sam that the device would sell successfully, but she herself was scracely convinced it could be mass-produced in a short time with large profits in mind.

It was a simple machine whose electric motor drove an intake fan which drew air through a specially designed filter and expelled it free of dust. Thanks to the properties of the fan mechanism, which were the work of Laura's brilliant and somewhat eccentric co-worker Randy Powers, the portable unit was capable of keeping an entire apartment free of dust for lengthy periods of time. Its removable filters, whose extraordinary sensitivity was Randy's greatest brainstorm, could be washed by hand, and were made of a synthetic material which dried with amazing speed after washing.

As Laura sat staring at the sketches her mind wrestled silently with the implications of the decision before her. Randy's clever invention, still only a promising prototype, might well be the answer to her company's prayers. But it had been one thing to lobby Sam for its manufacture. It was quite another to throw all the corporation's resources into this project on her own initiative. She alone would be responsible for its success or failure. It would be a calculated risk on which the fate of Christensen Products would hang; a risk Sam had refused to take even in happier times.

Nearly paralysed by the prospect of such personal accountability, Laura perused her own sales projections in tense silence. As the figures blurred before her eyes, her hand moved as though of its own volition and opened the company's xeroxed employee directory to Randy Powers' name. In a sort of concentrated daze she watched herself dial his phone number.

'Hello?' came an irritable voice.

'Hello, Randy,' Laura said into the receiver without taking her eyes from the plans before her. 'I'm at the office, and I was just wondering about something . . .'

'Laura? What are you doing downtown at this hour? You ought to be in bed. I'd be asleep myself, but I'm having a fight with my wife.'

'Give her my best, will you?' Laura murmured distractedly. 'Randy, I'd like to ask you a hypothetical question about our filter system. What do you think it would take to market it right away?'

'. . .'

The silence on the line was fimiliar to Laura. Randy was in the habit of falling into catatonic bemusement when a question took him by surprise.

'What I'm getting at,' Laura went on, 'is this. If we wished to sell this machine, say, in the spring, we could contract out the work on the plastic housing and on some of the motor parts. But the assembly would be up to us. I have a feeling our Springfield and Meriden plants could be refitted to take care of some of that work. But the next question is the filter. That's your design, and the essence of the machine's originality. Do you think you could set up the hardware to mass-produce that filter—say, right here in New Haven—in a matter of weeks?'

'Laura, there's nothing to that filter. You can buy the plastic from any synthetics company for five cents. It's how it's moulded.'

'I know. That's what I mean. Can you set up a shop here in town to mass-produce those filters?'

'Well, I don't know,' Randy yawned. 'That's not exactly my line. I dream the stuff up, and Sam—well, you, Laura—you'd have to get somebody to build the pressers and cut the filters and so forth. It could be done . . .'

'But to scale up your lab tools in order to mass-produce,' Laura persisted, 'would not be too tall an order for the Engineering Division, would it?'

'I don't see why it should,' Randy said. 'There's nothing that fancy about the mould . . .'

'One more thing, Randy,' Laura said, herself stifling an exhausted yawn. 'Is Shielah still working for her accounting firm?'

'Yes,' he growled. 'That's what we're fighting about. They're trying to transfer her . . .'

'And is Jason still in day care?'

'Where else would he be, with us both working?'

'Let me ask you one more question,' Laura said. 'With your combined incomes being what they are, how much would you be willing to pay for a portable machine that would free Shielah from having to dust the house?'

'I do the dusting, Laura.'

Laura smiled to think of Randy's punctiliousness. Though his labs at Christensen were always a mess, he kept his personal effects in a state of extravagent orderliness.

'Well,' she asked, 'how much would you pay for an item like that?'

'I don't know, Laura. Maybe seventy-five. Maybe a hundred. But I'm something of a cheapskate.'

'Thanks, Randy. And one more thing. I'm just looking at the time. Awfully sorry to call you so late. Tell Shielah I'm sorry I interrupted your fight.'

'Never mind. It was probably for the best. She's gone to bed now.'

'And kiss Jason for me. Goodnight, Randy.'

After replacing the receiver Laura sat in silence, her eyes closed. Inside her mind a slow revolution was taking place.

She had spent the last eight years of her life performing roles determined for her in advance—first as a college student, then as a corporation employee. Her personal contributions and ambitions had always been superseded by the larger entity of which she was a part.

Now, for the first time, she had an inkling of how Sam Christensen had felt as sole steward of his company's future. Rather than seek a place for himself in the world's existing structures, Sam had forced the world to make room for him through the products he invented and produced.

If Laura could inject Randy's dust removal system into the marketplace, people who had earmarked their household money for other purposes would change their minds and buy this new Christensen product. They would make room for it in a corner of their home or apartment. Competitors would try to duplicate it, paying royalties to Christensen for use of its patent.

Apartment dwellers without central air conditioning would have dust-free air for the first time. Homeowners could benefit equally. Thus an age-old problem would be solved for thousands, perhaps millions of consumers.

And if the product sold, Andrew Dillon and First Federal would have their short-term loans paid in full. Christensen's stock would go up quickly.

The order of things would have been changed. The world would have to make room for Christensen Products, rather than to absorb it.

Act, Frank Jordan had said. *Don't react. Make them react to you.*

For the first time in her life Laura understood what it meant to be a true executive, responsible for an entire company.

The feeling was both scary and wonderful.

Laura had arisen and reached to turn out the light when she recalled the sinister movements in her company's stock on Wall Street. Suddenly the lessons she had learned about corporate takeovers brought an idea to her mind with startling clarity. She left herself a note to call a number tomorrow morning, turned out the light, and moved exhaustedly towards the elevators.

On her way she left a memo for her secretary to schedule an urgent meeting with Randy Powers and Meg O'Connor, along with three of Christensen's materials and engineering managers.

And with Frank Jordan, she added on an after-thought.

As the office receded behind her she never thought to smile at the fact that Sam Christensen's tradition of nocturnal phone calls had just been restored.

Twenty minutes later she was home in bed, her somnolent body fighting for sleep against the plans thronging her mind.

Dream thoughts were beginning to vie with the probabilities and contingencies she weighed sleepily.

'We'll need a name for it,' she mused. 'Not Dustaway or No-Dust or anything prosaic like that. Something catchy. Something amusing and easy to remember—something to humanise the product.'

The image of an aged cleaning woman danced before her closed eyes. An irascible, temperamental lady who had worked for Sam when Laura was a little girl. The power struggle between employer and employee for control of the Christensens' domestic arrangements had led to an angry rift after less than a year, and the woman had left in disgust, calling Sam a fool and a hopeless mess-maker.

But Laura had liked her, for she had a pretty name: Molly Mahoney.

Molly, Laura thought with a smile.

Then she fell into a dreamless sleep.

CHAPTER FIVE

THE Directors' meeting took place on a rainy Wednesday afternoon. Rob Colwell held the door open for Laura, and gave her hand a furtive squeeze of encouragement as she entered the Board room. The seven members of Christensen's Board looked up expectantly at her through the haze of cigar and pipe smoke which filled the room.

Their faces were as foreign and as familiar as Sam's office, which Laura had occupied uncomfortably for nearly three weeks now. They were men in their fifties and sixties, stockholders and bankers whom she had known as a child, and to whom she had served cocktails at the Everit Street house when a teenager. A hint of their old avuncular smiles was visible on a face or two now, but most of them seemed to conceal their fears for the company under deadpan expressions.

Near the end of the table sat Frank Jordan in his capacity as non-voting observer and consultant. His eyes were upon Laura as well, their gaze intense and inscrutable. Laura thought she saw the shade of his familiar arrogance, as though Frank believed he was her true judge and adviser. Like an irritable director anticipating the audition of a struggling actor, he waited for her performance.

'Good afternoon, gentlemen,' Laura said, swallowing her emotions with an effort. 'Our first order of business, as you know, will be to confirm my nomination as President under the bylaws. Do I hear a motion to that effect?'

'So moved,' came Rob's voice.

'Seconded.'

The show of hands was unanimous, but rather bleak. Virginia recorded the result on her memo pad.

'Now,' Laura went on, 'we do have some important business to take care of today.'

All eyes were fixed on her, expectant and worried. By now it was common knowledge among the Board members that the company's falling sales dictated the cutbacks proposed by Zalman Corey. No doubt they were resigned to that fact, though unwillingly, for they all must feel that Sam would somehow have solved the problem of the company's debt. Laura could feel their larger fear that, over and above the immediate financial danger, her presence in the powerful role her father once played might bode ill for the corporation's whole future.

'I'm sure you're all aware,' she said with studied calm, 'that my father had been negotiating on a tentative basis with Paltron, Inc. of Massachusetts, with a view to Christensen's acquisition of that company.'

Eyebrows were raised around the table. Clearly everyone had expected Laura to open the meeting with the news that she would agree to close several Christensen factories. And here she was talking about acquisitions!

'I have spoken to John Slowicki and his colleagues at Paltron,' Laura said brightly, 'and I am happy to report that we have seen our way clear to close the deal. Christensen will acquire Paltron as of this week. The purchase price will be 750,000 shares of unissued Christensen common stock.'

Shock waves went silently through the room. Rob Colwell's features were clouded by perplexity. In a corner Zalman Corey sat pale as a ghost, his nervous hand adjusting the horn rims of his glasses. The Board members were staring at Laura, their lips pursed in blatant disapproval.

'And how do you propose to capitalise this idea?' asked Ralph Simpson, the oldest and most conservative member of the Board.

'Certainly not by closing our facilities in Rochester, Albany and Springfield,' Laura said frimly. 'Those plants will stay open at reduced capacity until we are able to bring them back to full production. We will finance the Paltron acquisition by divesting ourselves of some real estate properties which my father had acquired for just such a purpose as this. The unissued stock is already authorised. I might add, though, that each of us top Christensen executives will take a 20 per cent cut in salary as of next week. The inconvenience will be temporary, I can assure you.'

Angry mumbles of protest filled the room. Laura's actions seemed absurd, and quite irrelevant to the company's current woes as understood by the Board.

Only the face of Frank Jordan expressed a fugitive glimmer of approval. Laura's hooded glance in his direction acknowledged it.

'Now,' she said, 'let me end with some further good news. We are going ahead with a new project, tentatively called Molly. This consumer item was designed by Randy Powers of our Research Division. Virginia will pass out the projections we've done on it. The major electronic aspects of its assembly will be handled by Paltron in Massachusetts, with whom I have already discussed the situation.'

A pained silence had descended on the Board. Flabbergasted by Laura's unaccountable decisions, they stared at each other in bewilderment as Virginia placed the folders before them.

'We'll be doing some contracting for materials and parts manufacture,' Laura went on imperturbably. 'As you know, we can count on Rob Colwell's expertise in that area. As for finance and marketing, I will be personally involved, along with Frank Jordan and

Zalman Corey. We expect to be in production by the
end of February. I believe (*I pray*, she thought
silently) I can promise you and our shareholders a
strong first quarter and a brilliant second quarter of
the new year once this product hits the market.'

With her fingers crossed, Laura called for discussion
on her proposals. The shocked Board members, having
finally digested the enormity of the changes she was
suggesting, began to ask for clarification. For nearly two
hours she parried their questions, arguing carefully for
her plans while avoiding any reference to the desperate
motives which had made them necessary.

In the end Laura's own power as Board Chairman
and majority stockholder, combined with the clever-
ness of her arguments, won the day. The issue of
Christensen Products' imminent peril under the
pressure of its unseen adversaries was not discussed.
Only Frank Jordan shared that terrible secret with
Laura.

After the meeting Frank accompanied her to Sam's
office.

'Very smart,' he said when the door was closed
behind them. 'You've managed to create 750,000 new
shares of stock which will be in friendly hands at
Paltron. That will give you leverage against Schell in a
proxy fight. What gave you the idea?'

'Randy's system,' Laura said as she watched him
throw his jacket on a chair and loosen his tie. 'It
seemed smarter to acquire Paltron than to contract out
the electronic work to them. And, as you say, there
was the stock to consider.'

He had sat down in the chair opposite her, his long
limbs dwarfing its modest dimensions. Despite the
urgency of the moment, he seemed extraordinarily at
ease within himself, as though the drama that had just
drained Laura of her resources of guile and courage
were an everyday occurrence to him.

'There's one important thing you'll want to consider before the weekend,' he said. 'Under disclosure law you ought to report your acquisition of Paltron to the Stock Exchange right away. When Roy Schell hears about that, he'll know two things: that you have a big block of stock in friendly hands now, and that he may face anti-trust litigation if he tries to take you over now that you've already merged with a company in the same market.'

'I've already done that, Frank,' Laura said from Sam's chair.

'Well, well,' he smiled, his eyebrow raised in admiring surprise. 'You have been doing your homework, haven't you?'

Laura nodded, proud of her own initiative and more than a little flattered by his approval.

'Just to drive the point home more forcefully,' he added, 'a half-page announcement of the acquisition in the *Journal* might be a good idea. It will impress your stockholders as well as Schell and his friends.'

'Already done,' Laura said. 'The ad will be in Friday's edition.'

Frank crossed his arms and gazed across the desk at her, a trace of gentleness in his probing irises.

'I'll be damned,' he said. 'You're made of tougher stuff than I thought. So you believed me about Schell all along.'

'The movement of our stock on Wall Street doesn't lie,' Laura said. 'Someone is preparing to take us over. Whether it's Roy Schell or someone else, we have no choice but to fight now. In another month it might be too late.'

'You're taking a chance, you know,' he said. 'You're gambling everything on this product you call Molly. If it sells, and Christensen's stock goes up, Schell will give up and look for greener pastures. But if it doesn't sell, or moves too slowly, you'll be so overextended by

March or April that this company will be a sitting
duck. Doesn't that scare you?'

'Of course,' Laura said. 'But a certain amount of
fear goes with this job, unless I miss my guess.'

'You know something?' he asked, a laughing sparkle
in his caressing eyes. 'For a little slip of a thing, you
fill that chair pretty well.'

Laura felt herself flush under his gaze. Her weeks of
frantic work had convinced her that she was equal to
the tasks he had set her. But her memory of his hard
man's body, poised in that same visitor's chair the
night he stunned her with his warning words, had
dimmed in the intervening days, and was coming to
life in her senses now with fearsome immediacy. She
could see muscles strain under the white fabric of his
shirt as he clasped his hands behind his head. A lock
of his dark hair hung carelessly over the tanned flesh
of his brow. To hear him refer to her body, however
teasingly, sent an odd little quiver through her slender
limbs.

She had half accustomed herself to the mental image
of him as an arrogant tormentor bent on exhorting her
to bold actions of which he did not deem her capable.
But his grudging praise seemed to open the door to an
unforeseen view of him as a handsome, virile being
whose lips might attract one's own, whose powerful
limbs one might like to touch, to caress . . .

She banished the guilty thought with a shudder. But
the hot flush which had come over her creamy
complexion was worth a thousand words, and she had
to hope he would attribute it to mere modesty.

For his compliment had meant a lot, whether he
knew it or not.

'Now,' he said, reclining comfortably before her,
'why don't you tell me how you propose to get this
Molly of yours off the drawing board and into the
department stores by the first week in April?'

As she began to speak, the Board members had gone home to their respective institutions, thunderstruck by the boldness of their new Chairman and Company President. No one understood what she was up to, or knew how to stop her. Having expected her to accede docilely to the proposed closing of three Christensen factories, they were mystified by her decision to acquire Paltron and by the pay cut she had so imperiously imposed on Christensen's executives. Laura seemed to have received her marching orders from another world, a world foreign to their expectations and concerns.

But Laura was majority stockholder. No one could stop her in her tracks, for Sam had bequeathed her his power along with his shares. One could only swallow one's indignation and hope that she knew what she was doing.

'Hardly the way Sam did things,' one Board member grumbled to another in the elevator. His interlocutor shrugged a smile in answer, for he could recall many a surprise unveiled by Sam during Board meetings in years past. Perhaps, he mused, the girl was her father's daughter after all.

And they went their separate ways, never realising that under the guise of a routine acquisition and a new product line, a trench war against a corporate takeover had begun.

CHAPTER SIX

By early December Molly, the portable dust removal system designed to ease the odious household chores of millions of consumers, was no longer a drawing-board prototype in the bowels of Christensen Products' Research Division. It was a top priority for immediate production and test marketing, intentionally shrouded in mystery by the handful of planners Laura had assembled to hasten the process of its development.

Among them were Randy Powers and his hard-headed research colleague, Meg O'Connor. For the past several years Christensen insiders had called Meg Randy's 'better half', for it was Meg who knew how to cajole Randy from his eccentric, uncommunicative daydreaming and force him to put hard facts on paper for his superiors. A plump, cheerful woman in her early thirties, Meg had a sharp tongue and ready wit to match her bright red hair and sparkling eyes. Though Randy had tasted the sting of her Irish temper on more than one occasion, he knew she doted on him with maternal tenderness, and would protect him against those Christensen executives foolish enough to doubt the practical benefits of his seemingly inchoate designs.

Rob Colwell was in charge of materials for Molly's manufacture. Laura's contact with him during these hectic weeks had been mainly by telephone, for he was constantly travelling from one factory to another, examining plastics and metals whose characteristics must assure Molly's light weight and durability.

Laura well knew that Rob was anything but confident about her refusal to cut back Christensen's overhead and her huge investment of precious time and money in an untried product. Yet, once the die had been cast, Rob had responded to the new initiative with his accustomed aplomb. Upon his return from the far-flung outposts he visited in her behalf, Rob would appear in her office or meet her for lunch, his robust good looks seemingly accentuated by the busy routine he was now following. His reports were laconic and to the point, just as they must have been in Sam's time. He never failed to take every contingency into consideration, and his recommendations were always thoroughly researched. Laura thanked her lucky stars for his invaluable skills.

Rob had eyed Frank Jordan with ill-concealed suspicion after Laura dropped her bombshell at the Board meeting. Clearly his sharp intuition made him aware of Frank's influence on her decision, and he was concerned as to whether it was in her own best interests and those of the company. But his own business acumen must have told him there was solid strategy behind the bold moves Laura had undertaken. So he had turned in upon himself and gone about his work like the thorough professional he was. Laura even thought she sensed in him a grain of admiration for an idea he might have liked to have invented himself.

But the troubling atmosphere of tension between the two men, both so virile and incisive, seemed to persist underneath their polite exchanges, and might have become a real dilemma in itself had they seen more of each other. As things stood, however, Rob spent his days on aeroplanes destined for plants in Florida, Montreal, or Baltimore, while Laura and Frank kept their fingers on the pulse in New Haven.

In charge of finance for the urgent new project was Zalman Corey, who soon came to anticipate his new boss's nocturnal phone calls. Having immersed herself in the miasma of her company's liquid assets and

overheads, Laura importuned Zalman with one
financial gamble after another in her determination to
somehow underwrite Molly's production and distribution without crippling the corporation's overall
balance of payments. For Zalman, who much
preferred a quiet life with his wife and three cats, the
new routine was torture. Time and again Laura had to
use her hastily acquired financial expertise to reassure
him, when she inwardly wished it was he who might
calm her frayed nerves.

For her own part Laura supervised every aspect of
Molly's development, and did her best to hurry the
corporate process designed to make the new product
available to the public before the spring deadline
enforced by First Federal. Each morning she met with
her personal staff to apportion the day's labours.
There were phone calls to make, contingency plans to
collate and adjust, contracts to be signed, and new
strategies to discuss.

The most urgent priority was Molly's price. If the
machine could not be made affordable for financially
beleaguered apartment dwellers and homeowners, it
would never sell. Therefore every aspect of its
manufacture had to be scaled to the budget of the
middle-class consumer who had long since given up
expensive luxuries, but whose busy career made a
time-saving device like Molly an attractive item.

And the best way to spread the burden of Molly's
attendant overheads economically was to use as many
Christensen workers and plants as possible—along
with newly acquired Paltron—to make the item.
Outside contract work must be kept to a minimum.

To accomplish this purpose while simultaneously
overseeing the many other disparate activities in
Christensen's dozens of factories was a dizzying task.
More often than not, her head spinning, Laura felt as
though her ten fingers were trying to stop a hundred

holes in the massive dike that was Sam's company. For every phone call she made about Molly, five were coming in about other Christensen problems around the country. Through an effort of will she had to tell herself each night that her day's work would suffice until tomorrow, and that six or seven hour's sleep were more important than the piles of reports which conspired to keep her in her office until the wee hours of the morning.

'Hold on,' she told herself grimly. 'Just don't panic. Keep calm.' And she laughed to think that that was the most impossible thing of all to accomplish.

Sometimes her sense of humour abandoned her altogether, and she was convinced that each and every decision she had made was hopelessly inadequate. How comfortable it would be, she thought, to forget this miserable corporate rat race and live out one's days as a worker or teacher somewhere, unburdened by responsibilities one was incapable of handling.

At such moments Frank Jordan became the most important figure in Laura's life—and the most maddening.

Frank must have been keeping in close touch with Virginia about the rhythms of Laura's busy schedule, for he seemed to appear without an appointment just when she had a few moments to spare, or when his intuition told him her confidence must be particularly shaken by recent events.

Laura could hear the deep, confident tones of his voice as he bantered with Virginia in the outer office. In spite of herself she would glance hurriedly in the office mirror, touching her sandy hair with an urgent finger and cursing her silliness as she noticed the odd expectancy in the green eyes that looked out at her. A moment later he would appear at her door, his lips quirked by the wry smile she had come to expect, and throw his jacket unceremoniously over a chair.

'So,' he would say brightly as he sat down before her. 'Eveything under control?'

In his enigmatic eyes she often saw the same look of condescension that had so irritated her when he first joined the company. Mercilessly he seemed to tease her, indicating by his every word and gesture that she was in well over her head and was paying the painful price for Sam's ill-advised decision to thrust this enormous obligation upon her.

When she saw that look, her stung pride forced her to answer him with glib confidence, despite her fears. She found herself studying the intricacies of the company's structure, and the most remote fiscal calamities which might befall it, just so as to be able to stop Frank Jordan short with a witheringly competent reply when he tried to point up her inexperience and ignorance.

'I understand Engineering is helping Randy to refit the presses on our local lines,' he said one afternoon as he sat comfortably on the edge of Sam's desk. 'Don't you think you're going to have to do some extra hiring when he finishes? That will cost money.'

'Not if we use numerical controls on the machines,' Laura said with a straight face. 'Computer-linked, of course. My father bought and paid for the soft technology last year, so we might as well use it. Besides, we can retool for quality control whenever we like.'

When his brow raised in teasing admiration as he stared down at her, she was satisfied that once again she had passed his test.

Frank was a pitiless taskmaster. It was he who advised Laura on the budgeting of her time and that of her staff. With an uncanny instinct for executive planning, Frank explained what choice must be made first among the welter of options facing Laura at each stage of this complicated game. He seemed to possess an encyclopaedic knowledge of Christensen's own plants and suppliers to match the financial expertise he had brought from his years in what Sam had called a 'bigger pond', for none of Laura's reports on unsuspected problems in materials or assembly seemed to surprise him.

His aplomb amazed Laura. Thriving on pressure, taking everything in his stride, he managed to avert one crisis after another with unflappable calm. His coat thrown over his shoulder, his open collar revealing the crisp tangle of hair beneath his throat, Frank walked through the corridors of Christensen's headquarters like a relaxed tourist. Yet his sharp eyes missed nothing. At a moment's notice he straightened his tie, threw on his jacket, and was the image of daunting executive aggressiveness in the tense meetings that required his presence.

'He doesn't know what fear is,' Laura thought in wonderment as she contemplated him. 'Thank heaven.'

How she needed his peerless self-assurance at a time like this! The word troubleshooter could have been invented for him.

But he expected an equal daring from Laura herself, and was markedly impatient when she failed to show it.

In December Frank accompanied her to Christensen's Meriden facility. She watched intently as he entered into complex deliberations with the plant manager about strategies for mass-producing Molly's motor module at a minimum of expense.

'We can't handle this in the time frame you're talking about,' the worried manager said. 'We'd need too much overtime. The union won't hear of it.'

'Not if you fit smaller moulds into the lines you already have,' Frank said, his tanned hand pointing to a computer print-out he had brought with him from

New Haven. 'We'll make you the moulds in Albany next week. And Laura will talk to the union membership. Won't you, Laura?'

She nodded, making a show of confidence while wondering just how Frank expected her to negotiate with a union whose officials she had never met.

Yet, when she explained the profit-sharing plan devised by Frank and Zalman in anticipation of Molly's sales, the union reluctantly agreed to a temporary overtime arrangement at increased wages. Frank had been right again—if only because the membership remained loyal enough to Sam Christensen's memory to go along with his daughter's plans.

Frank's recommendations had in common the fact that they were easier said than done—and uniformly effective once put into place. Under his demanding guidance Laura found herself constrained to play the aggressive, self-possessed role her father had created for himself and passed on to her. More often than not she felt herself more an actress feigning executive competence than a true corporate leader.

But as time went on she found to her surprise that her carefully modulated performance seemed to rub off on her own personality. Catching a glimpse of her energetic, preoccupied face in the mirror, she saw traces of the change her new way of life was bringing about in her. The modest, unambitious research assistant she had once been was slipping quietly into oblivion, eclipsed by a woman accustomed, willingly or not, to being in charge of things and people.

And behind this change, Laura was well aware, loomed the mysterious figure of Frank Jordan. It was he who had forced her to seize the reins of her company, rather than to see it swallowed by forces beyond her control. It was he who had insisted that she follow her own initiative rather than to react to events.

As she sat in her father's office, surrounded by traces of his buoyant spirit, and acutely conscious that it was his furtive amendment to the bylaws that had put her here, she knew that Frank Jordan was somewhere in the building, planning things for her to do, challenges to which she must rise. It was becoming increasingly difficult to know where the one left off and the other began, for both summoned her incessantly to rise above herself.

But if Frank was satisfied with her progress, he took pains not to show it. His exhortations to bold action always had a hard edge, whether or not there was a hint of affection behind them. Sometimes he reminded her of a demanding coach who browbeats his talented athlete into living up to her potential, even at the cost of exhaustion and considerable acrimony. At other times she thought such a comparison too flattering to herself, for his supercilious glances left little doubt that he considered her a spoiled child deserving of sympathy only because she had been forced to sleep in the bed her father made for her. Eventually, he seemed to believe, she would certainly have to step down and turn her position over to someone competent. Until that time he would see to it that her inexperience did not destroy the corporation entirely.

And sometimes Laura was simply too tired to second-guess him. She took his indispensable advice at face value, and stopped asking herself whether he was making fun of her or honestly trying to encourage her. As he stood behind her chair, massaging her tired shoulders with strong, warm hands whose calming touch soothed her nerves, his very silence indicated that this short break must suffice to give her strength for more work.

The mystery of the man maddened her as much as his teasing ways. Nevertheless she welcomed the change he had brought about in her at a time when it was desperately needed. She had Frank Jordan to thank for the fact that Christensen Products still had a chance to survive and prosper.

Yet there was a dark side even to this state of affairs. For Frank was subtly making a new woman out of Laura. And that new woman, strengthened by adversity and tempered by new challenges, was far from indifferent to his charms. Even as the hard work he pushed upon her grew more satisfying, she found her senses responding tumultuously to the impact of his nearness.

Laura felt oddly out of place in her own skin, and frightened by a longing she had never experienced before.

The weather had grown colder, and the ocean breezes brought a preponderance of grim, rainy days to New Haven's tortuous maze of one-way streets. On regular occasions Frank joined Laura for lunch in the employees' cafeteria, or took her to dinner at a quiet restaurant near the Green. These encounters were intense affairs which seemed to rush by as the two sat absorbed in technical or financial discussion. Yet Laura could never entirely suppress her inner alertness to the physical side of Frank's virile personality. She noticed the clothes whose cut concealed the breadth of his back and shoulders, and the hard line of his jaw in which a tiny nerve quickened when circumstances darkened his mood.

And she came to admire the many resources of his humour, for he laughed easily when the complexities of their common work amused him. As though aware that the relentless pressure of her existence would be downright unhealthy if not interrupted at intervals, he insisted on celebrating each important step forward in Molly's evolution by bringing Laura flowers and ordering champagne at dinner. He seemed determined to throw a curtain of levity over the atmosphere of hectic gloom reigning in her life, for the more nerve-wracking things became, the more his acerbic wit found ways to make Laura laugh.

His cynicism about the business world perplexed Laura, for it harmonised poorly with the voracious love of life's varied challenges which shone forth in his every gesture and idea.

'If this is all just a "deadly game", as you called it,' she asked, 'why do you work so hard at it? Why are you putting so much effort into our problems at Christensen, when you could be doing something else?'

'The exception proves the rule,' he shrugged. 'Christensen is a damned good company. It makes products for people to use, instead of sacrificing everything to profit. That was your dad's work, and I'd like to see you carry it on. There aren't many companies like yours any more. The law of the jungle is money today, Laura. It makes for some interesting chess-playing with sharks like Roy Schell. And that amuses me. I want to see the look on Andrew Dillon's face when you pay off your short-term notes. I want to see Schell back off and look for another victim. In the end, it's their kind who will control the corporate world as a whole—but it's worth it to frustrate them this time.'

And he changed the subject with gentle determination, focusing his attention on Laura's own challenges while distracting her from himself.

But he could not have read the effect of his words in Laura's thoughts. To her they signified one thing only: that his tenure at Christensen Products was to be temporary. One day he would leave, putting the current battle behind him when it was won or lost, and continue his adventurous career elsewhere.

And when he left, would he take away a part of her

that she could never recover?

Laura needed Frank Jordan now, more than she had needed anyone since Sam was alive. But underneath her prideful irritation at her dependence on him, she wanted to need him. Yes, she mused uncomfortably: a part of her cried out to give itself to Frank forever, so that she could spend all her days enfolded by the vital charm of his body and personality. And that persistent little part added its disturbing voice to all her other thoughts when he was near. Even as she asked herself what he wanted from her today, how he might help her through her newest crisis, a furtive inner voice asked, *Does he like me? Does he find me attractive?*

In consternation she suppressed the thought. But when next his smiling face appeared at her office door, its handsome features quirked in sharp, wry humour, that prohibited yielding in her senses came to taunt her anew.

It had been one thing to swallow her pride and accede to his harsh, threatening demands, cursing his impudent behaviour even as she admired the analytical mind which saw so clearly into the heart of her company's dilemma.

It was quite another to find her consciousness bound insidiously to the vibrant image of his tanned flesh, hard and sure, drawing closer to her with the same quick expertise that guided his steps in the perilous world of men, covering her luxuriantly, overwhelming her with its caress.

'Don't,' she told herself angrily. 'Don't even think about it.'

But when she looked inside herself in search of an answer to her own confusion, it was Frank Jordan's dark gaze that seemed to look out at her, holding her in rapt fascination.

CHAPTER SEVEN

FRANK had warned Laura that the key to Molly's short-term success would be an aggressive advertising campaign.

'I like the name,' he said. 'It's cute—and since the product is not exactly poetic in itself, we should humanise it. But the problem is that we're trying to sell people on the *idea* of Molly, as well as our specific product.'

After consultation with Christensen's advertising department, Laura was tempted to launch Molly through full-page ads in mass-market publications. Her advisers wrote a tentative text describing the machine's virtues.

'I don't think so, Laura,' Frank said with a frown. 'This sort of campaign won't convince anyone to take a chance on what amounts literally to a new invention. We need something more immediate. Something to grab people's attention and make them feel that Molly is the product they've been waiting for all these years. I think television is the only answer. It will be expensive, but worth it. We have to reach a lot of consumers quickly. After that has been accomplished we can go to magazines to bolster the impact of the initial campaign.'

The logic behind Frank's suggestion was convincing, but neither Laura nor the advertising staff could decide on an appropriate manner of presenting Molly in a television commercial. The little machine was not unattractive to look at, but was hardly photogenic in itself. Nothing about it offered possibilities for visual excitement, for it was designed to do its work quietly and unobtrusively.

There was no gainsaying the obvious: despite its amusing name, Molly was downright dull. In Frank's words, something must be done to make the product human.

One evening Laura lay somnolent on the couch before the television set in her apartment. On the screen was an old Hollywood movie depicting the stormy relationship between an eccentric millionaire and his uncontrollable children. The only sensible person in his opulent mansion seemed to be an irascible housemaid who reigned over the place like a friendly tyrant. Dressed in black with an abbreviated white apron, she excoriated her whimsical employer in blunt, strident terms when events forced him into hilariously ill-considered behaviour. She saw through all the story's characters, easily distinguishing those who were merely foolish from those whose motives were genuinely suspect. Often she expressed her judgments through subtle looks whose import was always borne out by the story.

Something stirred in Laura as she contemplated the matronly actress, whose face was as familiar as her name was unknown to the public. For decades she had played the role of the gruff, hardheaded housekeeper to perfection.

Instinctively Laura placed a videotape in the cassette recorder she had inherited from Sam and began taping the movie. When it was over she studied the list of players carefully. The name Marva Sims struck a distant chord in her memory.

The next morning Laura called Francie Tolliver, a bright young executive in the advertising department, and asked her to come to Sam's conference room. As Francie watched, Laura played portions of the tape she had recorded the night before.

'Watch Flora, the maid,' she said. 'Look at her authority. She's the only character who understands the household.'

'Her carriage is wonderful,' Francie murmured, her brow furrowed in concentration. 'So erect. She seems a tower of strength. Who is she?'

'Her name is Marva Sims,' Laura said. 'I have no idea whether she's living. That film is at least thirty years old. But it's the idea that intrigues me. A clever, competent housekeeper who not only understands dusting and housework, but who is a shrewd judge of people.'

'You mean as a visual spokesman for Molly,' Francie said, tapping a pencil lightly against her briefcase as she watched the screen. 'I see what you're getting at.'

'Francie, I'd like you to do something for me. Leaving Marva Sims aside, if we could find someone like her someone whose image is associated with good common sense ... A character actress with a recognisable face.'

'We could show her as insisting that her employer buy her a Molly so that she could devote herself to more important work than mere dusting,' Francie said. 'Personally, I can't think of anyone who plays that sort of role regularly nowadays, but I'm sure I can find out. A little leg work with the casting agencies ...'

'Exactly,' Laura said. 'I appreciate your help, Francie. And remember: we don't have much time to spare. I'm convinced that Molly needs a human image, and a strong one. A person people can identify with.'

When Francie had gone Laura returned to the conference room cassette recorder to rewind the tape. As the black-and-white film disappeared from the television screen replaced by a raucous game show, she reached hurriedly to turn down the volume. As luck would have it, the knob came off in her hand. In irritation she reminded herself that the TV set was growing old and must soon be replaced. Only a few weeks ago Virginia had sent it to the repair shop for work on its outmoded tubes.

A tiny glint of soldered metal caught her eye on the volume control post as she tried to replace the knob. She gazed distractedly at it for a moment, wondering whether it signified one of the repairman's efforts to keep the old set in working order.

A sudden glimmer of doubt told her the thing made no sense. The melted solder was shiny and new, and could have no place on a purely mechanical part of the controls. On an impulse she borrowed the magnifying glass from Virginia's desk drawer and returned to the silent conference room.

Recalling the lessons she had learned in microtechnology as a research specialist, Laura peered through the glass. A moment's careful scrutiny revealed a tiny circle of tooled metal nestled in the droplet of hardened solder. Barely visible to the naked eye, the device clearly had an electrical function and a purpose all of its own.

The improbable truth struck Laura all at once.

It was a microphone.

Loath to believe her own eyes, she knelt before the set, her finger keeping her long hair from her face as she stared at the minuscule contrivance. For weeks she had reluctantly accustomed herself to the notion that Christensen Products was the object of acute attention on the part of unseen strangers. But this almost microscopic evidence of a deliberate invasion of her own privacy and that of her colleagues seemed unutterably sinister.

So they care that much, she thought angrily, taking care not to put the idea into words.

She stood up and moved quickly towards her office, intending to use the telephone. But she was stopped in her tracks by the fear that that room was no more secure than this.

A moment later she was hurrying through the corridor towards the elevators, answering her co-workers' salutations with a forced smile.

She had to find Frank Jordan.

Two days later a dour group of top Christensen executives met in the conference room to discuss the discontinuing of three important product lines and the prospective sale of two Christensen factories.

'I think we're all in agreement,' Rob Colwell said from his position beside Laura, 'that the pay cut decided on at the Board meeting last month was necessary. However, it doesn't seem to have helped us that much.'

'I'm sure our shareholders will appreciate it,' Laura said.

'Yes, but the executive pool isn't happy about it,' Frank Jordan put in. 'I think there's a strong chance that we'll see some of our people looking for opportunities elsewhere.'

'I don't see what choice we had,' Laura said hesitantly. 'I'm sure it will only be temporary, Frank. Once we divest ourselves of some overhead and take care of our short-term debt, we'll readjust salaries accordingly. But for now a little belt-tightening seems the only safe course.'

'I agree,' Rob shrugged. 'We have to be conservative, particularly in the wake of the Paltron acquisition.' His voice betrayed a hint of reproach at what he obviously considered an ill-advised move. 'We'll just have to hope that sales pick up in the last two quarters of the new year. If they do, Christensen will be a stronger company, if a somewhat smaller one.'

'In the meantime,' Frank said, 'morale is an important issue, Laura, I think you should try to make this year's Christmas party the best in a long time.

And some sort of bonus across the board would be a welcome token of appreciation for our people. Even if you have to squeeze blood from a turnip to do it, you should free enough cash to put a little something in everyone's Christmas envelope.'

A wry smile curled his lips as he looked from the page before him to Laura. Rob's eyes were on the silent television set, their tawny irises glinting with suppressed humour.

'Zalman,' Laura said, 'this is your field. Do you see a way for me to give out bonuses at all comparable to what we had last year?'

Zalman adjusted his glasses nervously. He alone seemed oblivious to the concealed hilarity filling the room.

He was concentrating on his script.

CHAPTER EIGHT

'LAURA, how much of your French do you remember?'

Frank stood tall at Laura's office door, his coat thrown over the shoulder of the thick sweater which hugged the contours of his powerful chest and arms. The taut thighs under his slacks accentuated his aura of alert animal strength coiled for quick and efficient action. Looking up from her desk Laura was momentarily struck dumb by her sheer admiration for his exuberant male authority.

'My French?' she asked in confusion. 'I don't know. I suppose I could still read a newspaper. Or perhaps order a cup of coffee in a restaurant.'

'You'll have to do better than that,' he smiled, throwing his coat on the chair beside the window. 'I've just had a chat with Zalman Corey. You and I are going to Montreal on Friday. Rob Colwell will meet us there. We have to arrange to manufacture Molly in Quebec. And you know how some of those Québeçois feel about English these days.'

'Frank, are you sure about this?' Laura sighed. 'Can't we just export to Canada?'

'Not the way things are today,' he shook his head. 'With exchange rates and import duties the way they are, the product won't be affordable. We have to build and distribute it in Canada. It's going to be a gamble, because the Canadian operation won't be ready to go until late spring at the earliest. But we ought to lay the groundwork right now. Rob called this morning, and he has a plant in mind. Once we've had a look at it, we can set the wheels in motion. And,' he added with a smile, 'we can mix business with a little pleasure for a

change. I know a terrific French restaurant up there,
and we might get in a morning of skiing before we
have to get back. What do you say?'

'Why not?' Laura laughed. 'I can just as easily have
a nervous breakdown in French as in English.'

'That's the spirit,' he joked, his ebony irises resting
on the tawny swirl of her hair. 'Virginia has the
reservations made. We'll leave Friday morning from
Laguardia.'

A moment later he had disappeared, for an urgent
meeting with Meg O'Connor and Randy Powers was
to fill the rest of his morning. Laura sat alone behind
her father's desk, her every fibre stunned by the
fugitive trace of Frank's caressing glance.

Though Frank Jordan apparently remained unaware
of the tormenting upset his nearness was causing in
Laura's senses, she herself had come perilously close
to breaking under the strain of her frayed emotions
these past weeks. Frank's erect virility, once a mere
image of tempting male attractiveness before her
mind's eye, had expanded insidiously to overwhelm
her imagination. It was increasingly difficult to
concentrate on the urgent tasks he persisted in
bringing her when his every glance, the casual touch
of his hand on her arm, his earthy male scent as he
leaned close to her, tore at the heart of her resistance
to his charms.

At first the intensity of her attraction to him had
been a sly little imp that teased and taunted her when
he was near. Feeling her knees go weak when he
helped her on with her coat, his strong fingers
brushing her back in their passage, she had tried to
enjoy the private thrill which stole under her skin, as
though it were nothing more than a furtive,
momentary impression.

But now it was different. Now the vital, athletic
form of Frank Jordan pursued her throughout her

busy day, and haunted her dreams at night. Each time
he arrived to take her to lunch or to a meeting, she
realised with a shock that his handsome face and
powerful body had not been out of her thoughts since
last she saw him.

Though his cynical disapproval of her high position
still peeked out occasionally from behind his friendly
treatment of her, it was now clear to Laura that his
respect for her initiative and hard work was sincere. In
his careful, vigilant way he had come to like her as a
person. True, she remained the mere pretext for the
battle he had joined in her company's behalf, but
something in his protective amiability told her that his
bitterness about the corporate world did not extend to
Laura herself. Frank Jordan had become her friend as
well as her ally.

But friendship was the extent of his feeling for her.
Of that Laura was convinced. Over and over again,
through these tumultuous weeks, she had found
herself taking extra care with her make-up, in the
unspoken hope that an extra glow in her cheeks, a
touch of colour above her limpid green eyes, would
make her more attractive to Frank. Unconsciously she
chose dresses, skirts and blouses whose trim and cut
might make her appear a bit more feminine at work.

She cursed her own fruitless wiles, for Frank's wry
gaze never lingered for long on the outfits designed to
highlight her slim good looks. The bright compliments
he offered were paternal in nature, and were obviously
intended to encourage rather than to flatter. In his
mind she was still the 'slip of a girl' whose fate had
decreed that she try to grow into a big and difficult job.

To make matters worse, Frank always seemed to
appear in her office at the very moment when her
exhausting day's work had left her hair in tangled
disarray, her make-up far from entrancing, her eyes
dull with fatigue. Hoping in her guilty heart to attract

his male interest, she succeeded only in appearing rumpled and ordinary when he approached.

Yet she could not stop herself from dreaming of him. Behind every hurried executive decision she made, behind every withering fear she felt for the future of her father's corporation, there lurked a secret eagerness for Frank's touch and smell, for his deep voice and sharp, knowing smile.

She had begun to feel herself a covert expert on every visible part of his handsome body, for her sidelong glances rested in fascination on the sinews of his neck, the hard length of his thighs, the curious glint of midnight blue in his dark eyes. She knew the ebony waves of his hair with an obsessive sureness. His body was becoming her personal talisman, filled with a dark allure that infuriated her. The wicked pleasure she took from the sight of it, when he took off his jacket to throw it on her chair, when he rolled up his sleeves for work, when he stretched his long limbs in moments of relaxation, was unbearably delicious.

But more disturbing yet was her idealisation of his image when she contemplated it in solitude. She had come to admire him with an adolescent's fervour, and found herself coveting every aspect of her familiarity with him. His voice on the telephone was a prized possession, and she listened to its deep tones with stealthy attention, wanting to know him better, to know all about him. In her girlish thoughts he had a stellar brilliance, a particular essence to which she clung selfishly despite her best efforts to put him out of her mind.

'Am I falling in love with him?' she wondered, shocked by the novelty of these strange feelings.

No eventuality could be more silly, more immature. In experience, if not in years, he was far too old for her. She would never be more to him than Sam's young daughter, a helpless creature he wished to protect from financial sharks he hated. Even the blithe, joking consideration he showed her seemed to confirm that he thought himself worlds apart from her, that he reserved his amorous attentions for more sophisticated women he knew in New York or elsewhere.

Perhaps he had an intense love life of his own. A long-term affair ... Perhaps he was a divorcé: Laura had never thought to inform herself on the subject.

She dared not admit to herself in all candour that it was love that inflamed her towards Frank Jordan. He was too enigmatic a figure, she told herself, to touch the centre of her woman's emotions. Ever since her youthful crush of Rob Colwell she had thought of true, adult love in terms of candour and trust. Charmingly outspoken as he was, Frank kept his feelings hidden behind the curtain of his indefatigable energy. If Laura had a place in his thoughts, he would have given her a sign of some sort, rather than to withhold himself so coolly.

Nevertheless, the dark intensity of his demeanour seemed to soften imperceptibly when he was alone with Laura. Occasionally he would take her hand with quiet affection, straighten an unruly lock of her sandy hair, his finger lingering for an instant on the downy surface of her cheek, a curious light of sympathy in his dark eyes.

At those moments the raw eruption in Laura's senses deepened vertiginously, and she told herself that love alone must be the source of the irresistible trust she felt for him.

Laura was living a contradiction, and its intensity was becoming unbearable. Frank Jordan had taught her a new self-reliance, and yet it was he whose initiative and expertise were responsible for the strides her company had made since Sam Christensen's death. And the more Laura felt herself capable of handling the company's future on her own, the more she doubted that her own future could contain a moment's happiness if Frank Jordan were not part of it.

Yet Frank manifestly took no notice of the feelings he kindled in her—feelings which grew each day in power and urgency, so that she felt she must die of frustration or throw herself at him with shameless abandon before another week was out.

As time grew short for Christensen Products, the fuse in Laura's emotions burned shorter and shorter as well. She knew its final flare would unleash a storm over which she would have no control.

The early flight to Montreal on Friday enabled Laura and Frank to meet Rob at an industrial park where Pirot et Cie. possessed a facility capable of producing the Molly in a matter of months. Rob had done his work well. Pirot's managers had already studied the blueprints he had brought, and concluded not only that there was a strong market for the product in Canada, but also that its cost could be held to a minimum by using existing machinery for production.

By late afternoon the major points of Christensen's leasing arrangement with Pirot had been ironed out. Amazed at the relative ease of the transaction, Laura and Frank were in a celebrative mood. Rob declined their invitation to join them for the evening, saying he had to fly back to New York for a luncheon meeting tomorrow. With a glance at Laura and a quick nod to Frank, he took his leave.

The executives at Pirot having surprised Laura by speaking to her in colloquial English without the trace of an accent, she had her first serious opportunity to speak French with the taxi driver whose vehicle bore her and Frank through the mad whirlwind of Montreal's traffic towards their hotel. To her amazement the small, dark man not only understood her hesitant questions about the unfamiliar city, but seized upon them as pretexts for airing his separatist political views. Though his pronounced accent and slangy turn of phrase made his disquisition difficult to understand, Laura gleaned that he blamed the government of Canada for all his city's problems. Delighted to hear that his passengers planned to manufacture a new product in his beloved province, he insisted on writing down its description, and promised to buy his hard-working wife a Molly when it became available.

Chez Victor, the French restaurant Frank had mentioned, was everything he had claimed it to be, although the ambience within its cramped confines was hardly what Laura might have expected. Only the flowers and fine silverware on its smattering of old tables suggested that it was anything more than a country-style *auberge*. The mimeographed menu handed out unceremoniously by a smiling, portly hostess was scrawled in a very French hand, and it was the chef-owner, M. Fasquelle, who appeared in his soiled apron to take orders from his well-to-do clients, whom he treated with grunting familiarity. His personal suggestions for dinner were communicated in so imperious a manner that Frank accepted them respectfully, his hooded glance at Laura glinting with amusement.

As it turned out, the blandly named terrine du chef, soupe de poissons, and boeuf à la moelle were culinary miracles whose subtlety and grace astounded Laura. For the first time in many weeks she found herself possessed of a genuine appetite, and Frank laughed to see her eat so heartily.

'Well,' he smiled as she somehow found room for the poire Belle Hélène which closed the meal, 'now I know how to put some flesh on that emaciated frame of yours. All I have to do is fly you up here every week-end.'

'I've been too worried to eat for so long,' Laura sighed. 'But I think under the worst of circumstances this place would make me hungry. It's a marvellous restaurant. Thank you for bringing me here.'

After another hurtling taxi ride through the city's frigid, windswept streets, they found themselves in the gleaming lobby of the hotel, behind whose shimmering drapes the lights of Montreal illuminated the night sky. The large, carpeted room echoed with the smooth strains of dance music from the adjacent lounge.

'I'll tell you what,' Frank said suddenly. 'We've had a good day, and we ought to finish it off with a little more celebration, if you're not too tired. Why don't we have a nightcap?'

The lounge was dark and lovely, its recessed lights glowing in corners decorated in subtle pastel greens. A few couples moved slowly on the dance floor while a trio played romantic songs in long, rhythmic phrases.

The brandy Frank ordered sent waves of delightful warmth through Laura's tired limbs. It had been a perfect day whose accomplishments, for a change, had not been marred by false starts and unpleasant surprises, and all at once Laura felt a curious surge of excited energy in all her senses.

'You know something?' Frank asked, his impish smile glimmering in the shadows. 'We can't go on like this, Laura.'

'What do you mean?' she asked, blushing in her perplexity.

'Just sitting here,' he said, 'without dancing, while all those people are enjoying themselves. You're the most beautiful woman in the room, and I should be showing you off.'

'Frank, I . . .' Despite his joking tone, his words

sent a thrill of expectation through Laura's body, and she felt suddenly diffident.

'Come on, now,' he insisted, taking her hand to lead her to the dance floor. 'This is a special night.'

The enfolding touch of his warm, dry hand, abetted by the brandy which tingled calmingly in her senses, sent a flood of yielding through her mind. All at once the most logical thing in the world seemed to simply place herself in his hands and forget the frantic emotions that had been tormenting her for weeks.

There was infinite gentleness in the strong body that led her in time with the quiet music. Frank's arm encircled her waist with easy familiarity, and her face drew close to his deep chest. She moved with him in a sort of charmed somnambulism, as though the dance itself were an impalpable element in which one could float without awareness of one's steps or of the song one heard.

She felt his hand graze her shoulder, her neck, her hair, in little strokes which had a magical power to silence the thoughts which troubled her happiness. The hardness of his thigh brushed her flesh soothingly, naturally. Though he held her with an almost ethereal softness, it seemed that this nearness of his tall, strong body was a steadfast edifice that buoyed her, lifted her liltingly atop swelling waves of sound and rhythm.

She was in his hands now, she told herself, and somehow their calm caress knew how to resolve the contradiction haunting her feelings for him—as though he knew how to be her ally, her friend, her protector, and also a strong, sensual man who could enjoy touching and holding her without insult to the mutual respect which was the essence of their relationship. And as he pulled her closer to the hard length of his body, so that his clean male scent suffused her senses, this bewitching contact itself seemed peaceful and secure, and not at all disturbing.

'That's my girl,' he murmured, the hard line of his jaw touching her temple. 'You do know how to relax, don't you?'

She nodded dreamily, lulled by the deep tones of his voice and by the delicate embrace which enfolded her.

And her sense of perfect well-being might have gone on indefinitely, had not a subtle flow of forces begun to tip her head backward—not so that her half-closed, unseeing eyes might contemplate him, but so that her soft lips might open to him, to accept his kiss with a great sigh of pleasure . . .

She arrested the impulse with a shock, unnerved to feel her body move with a will of its own when once her waking mind had relaxed its vigilance. And now it seemed that Frank's quiet touch was indeed an innocent and friendly thing, but that her own traitorous flesh could not be trusted to accept this intimacy without clamouring to make of it something more heated and insidious.

He had seen the rapt look in her eyes, and was smiling down at her as the song ended.

'My poor Laura,' he laughed. 'You're out on your feet. Let's get you upstairs to bed.'

Thank heaven, she thought in sudden panic. Thank heaven he had misunderstood. It was better this way, better that he should mistake her shamelessness for mere fatigue.

The elevator was sparsely filled with tourists and businessmen. Laura stood by Frank's side, still charmed by his relaxed cheer despite the tumult which had only begun to ebb in her senses. Her sidelong glances seemed to confirm that he had not noticed the effect he had had on her only moments ago.

But as they walked along the hushed, carpeted hallway towards her room, once again a great surge of warring thoughts overcame her. In a trice he would say goodnight, disappear to his own room and leave

Laura to her confused, taunting dreams. Bitterly she longed for the day when, for better or worse, Frank Jordan would get out of her life. Simple loneliness would be preferable to this agony of wanting he kindled in her without being aware of it himself. So magnetic was he that it was torture to be in the same room with him, close enough to touch him with eager hands, and yet separated from him by an impenetrable gulf of her own making.

The door opened and she turned to say goodnight. In a frightening flash she visualised herself seducing him, throwing herself at him shamelessly, pulling him into her bed. The idea was so disturbing that she feared her last words to him tonight would be spoken in a voice shaken by desire.

'Now,' he said quietly. 'You're a lady with a lot of responsibilities, and you need a good eight hours' sleep. I don't want you to get out of bed until I call you. Then we'll have a nice breakfast and see what the day holds for us.'

His hands were on her shoulders. As he bent to kiss her cheek, she felt her fingers grasp his long arms with a hesitant languor she could not control. His lips touched her softly and receded as her eyes half-closed in involuntary delight.

But her slender hands had not released him, and it was with an inner sigh of resignation that she let her eyes rest pleadingly upon his own, her irises glowing pale green in the shadows as a nearly imperceptible tremor in her touch told him what she wanted.

She saw the sudden gravity in his gaze, the quick alertness which saw into her soul, the inevitable quirk of surprise and perhaps disapproval which frowned in his dark brow.

Then the door began to close, and she thought her heart would burst with wanting.

For she was in his arms at last, her slender form

pressed full length against the hardness of his body by powerful arms locked firmly behind her back.

His kiss took her breath away, for it probed suddenly to the core of the heat she had vainly fought for so many days, allowing it to expand and carry her away in its triumph.

Somehow her hand must have found its way to the light switch, for a calming darkness engulfed her, banishing her long weeks of silent struggle with a sort of finality. At last she felt she could relax into the joy that was about to be hers, and she let her lips and tongue return the kiss that held her.

Awed by the terrible intimacy of that single kiss, so probing, so secret, she felt she belonged to him already. Her tongue met his own in a lithe dance of discovery, exploring and inviting. Her senses leapt dizzyingly as she felt his calm hands caress the soft curves they had never touched before. Their movement was unhurried, rhythmic, and the flesh of her back, her hips, her thighs came alive in little shivers of ecstasy under his caress.

She felt the ripple of his hard muscles under her fingertips as she pressed her hands to his back. With a sort of heedless joy she touched his neck, his broad shoulder. Her body moulded itself to his own, yielding in its every hollow to his hard flesh so that he would know she wanted him closer yet. Stunned by her own forwardness, she nevertheless exulted to feel his caress grow stronger, more heated.

So marvellous was this embrace which seemed to greet her body affectionately, lovingly, as after a long and painful separation, that she thought it might go on forever, inexhaustible in its perfection. But with a sigh she realised that her dress had come loose under his stroking fingers, her bra hung loose over the hand that grazed her breasts. And now, before she could quite realise that only her sheer panties still clung to her soft skin in the darkness, he was bearing her through the still air, placing her on the silky spread which slipped under her naked body.

She had not allowed herself to wonder what the reality of Frank Jordan's unclothed limbs might be. Now she lay in rapt anticipation as the muted sounds of his movements in the obscurity told her he was preparing to come to her. And it was with a little gasp of pleasure that she felt herself encircled by his long arms and gathered against the warm expanse of his nudity. The harsh power of his body did not daunt her, for he knew how to harness and tame it, so that it cradled her gently even as its earthy touch and smell drew her to caress and kiss it in avid fascination.

His lips closed softly over the hard nipple poised for their approach. A spasm of ecstasy stirred her as she held him to her breast, her fingers buried in his thick hair. Languorously her silken thighs moved under him, slipping against his hips, sending messages of eager yielding to his coiled senses.

She shuddered to feel him strip away the last flimsy fabric separating him from her, and grasped him more urgently as her naked skin breathed the charged air of the room. Great billows of passion surged through her slender limbs as he explored every part of her, the gentle enquiry of his lips and hands teasing her to a mad height of wanting.

And even as he joined himself to her at last, the power of him forcing sighs of rapture from her lips, there was a core of quiet mystery in the body whose slow movements drove her to a wild excitement she had never imagined possible in all her guilty dreams about him. Leaving no trace of her unexplored, overwhelming her with the hot flare of his own need, he nevertheless held her intact, safe from harm in his embrace. Thus she could grip him, clutch him to her, fill her senses with him until she thought she would burst, for his touch never violated her.

But there was no time to wonder at the strangeness of this fiery intimacy with an unknown man who gave of himself so freely, so sweetly, from the very depths of his unseen heart; for already her passion was preparing to spend itself in the silent room. The great spasms which shook her seemed to rend the very fabric of her life, so that its countless days and hours were banished in a trice, and in their stead loomed a single face, filling her body and soul with the dark magic of its knowing gaze.

When all was still inside her once more, and she lay in his embrace, her gasps of pleasure having slowed to somnolent rhythms of blessed rest, she allowed herself to dream that she belonged to him now, forever. The part of her mind that knew he remained a separate being, come from an unknown past and destined for a future perhaps far from her, slept first. For a long moment her rapt imagination clung to its conviction that this calm closeness was forever.

Then she was asleep in his arms.

CHAPTER NINE

THE grey glow of dawn brightened gradually as the heavy boom of delivery trucks in the streets outside signalled the awakening of the metropolis.

Laura lay in silence, her eyes fixed upon Frank's sleeping form. Admiration for his handsome face in repose vied with a sort of awed fascination in her regard, as though she were contemplating an untamed and dangerous being whose awakening would be a thing to be dreaded.

Frank Jordan was no less a contradiction this morning than he had been last night, in those agonising hours preceding the charmed instant when he had kissed her for the first time. His unknown thoughts were as penetrating and alert as the taut body which had cradled her in its embrace only hours ago. But the change he had wrought in Laura could never be undone.

Here he lay in his quiet sleep, dark and inscrutable, far from her in the exterior world. Yet her whole body still bore the daunting traces of the enormous intimacy she had shared with him. And never again would she be able to contemplate him coolly, to wonder detachedly about his past, his desires, his plans. He was inside her mind now, and she could no more re-establish her previous view of him than one can turn back the clock.

She shuddered to think that he could have made such a difference in her by simply gratifying the passion he had inspired during weeks of apparently workaday coexistence. What must he think of her now? Did her image have a place somewhere in the dreams that passed through his sleep? Would he awaken to smile down upon her with a trace of contempt for her childish forwardness?

Laura suddenly knew all the shame of her vulnerability. He had given her the intimacy she craved so violently, and now she must pay the consequences. He could think what he liked of her now, and imagine himself possessed of some sort of ascendancy over her if he wished. Indeed, he had had his way with her all these weeks. Had she not done his bidding in nearly every detail of her struggle to save Sam's company from disaster? It was Frank who had pulled the strings from his obscure position behind the scenes.

Perhaps, already amply convinced of Laura's naiveté and girlish simplicity, he had long been aware of her guilty feelings for him, and had decided on a whim that no great harm would be done to Christensen Products if he mixed business with his own pleasure for once. Perhaps it seemed convenient and even amusing for so experienced a man to take pity on the callow girl he had condescended to help in her emergency.

If that were the case, he would undoubtedly awaken to his own impatient fear that, having thrown herself at him like an adolescent, she would now presume to importune him with childish displays of possessiveness, as though in her romantic mind last night's lovemaking had meant something deep and permanent.

These thoughts stole painfully through her mind even as her glance lingered involuntarily over the strong, hard lines of Frank's sleeping body. And as she caught herself furtively recalling the ecstasy she had known in his arms, she felt more shamed than ever, and closed her eyes with a little spasm of determination.

'Don't,' she heard a low murmur which shocked her.

He was gazing at her sleepily, a smile on his lips.

'Don't look away,' he said.

'How did you know I was . . .?'

'I could feel your eyes on me,' he said. 'It was nice.'

And with a calm softness which amazed her, he extended a long arm to draw her close to him. Reluctantly she allowed her naked body to nestle in his warm embrace, and listened to the rhythm of his breathing, her face pressed to his deep chest.

For a long, lovely moment he held her that way as sleep dissipated in his vital body. She could feel the energy of the new day coming to life under the warm skin that grazed her own. The hand that rested on the curve of her hip was dry and relaxed. His fingertips brushed lightly at the billowed maze of her hair, and it was with a thrill of recognition that she felt his lips touch her temple, her earlobe.

'Sleep well?' he murmured, an impalpable smile in his voice.

She nodded, her lips against the crisp hair of his chest.

'That's my girl,' he said, his hands running gently over her back. 'A good sleep was what you needed. A woman can't run a big company on strung-out nerves, can she?'

Against her better judgment she let herself luxuriate in the protective cradle of his limbs. Now that she had given herself to him he seemed more thoughtful and considerate than ever. His awareness of what had happened between them shone only in this warm, silent intimacy of his naked body which enfolded her so naturally.

Yet it was disconcerting to feel so at home in his arms, when her scruples about what she had done still thronged her mind. And perhaps he sensed the doubt which tensed her sleepy limbs, for he gathered her closer to him, his hands moulding her body to his own as though to protect her from her own thoughts.

How marvellous it was to feel herself wedded to his own nudity, even for one charmed moment! She could imagine a lifetime of such magic, and in her mind's eye she saw herself joined to Frank Jordan forever by bonds of trust and intimacy. What would happen, she wondered, if she could wake up every morning in his arms? What challenges could frighten her then?

But the dream vanished as quickly as it had come, and she cursed her wishful thinking. Her woman's intuition made her suspect the pious impulse towards trust and dependency that comes after an unforgettable night of love. She was still a responsible adult, and bound by her own maturity to behave like one. What had happened left behind it no obligation on Frank's part. Were she foolish enough to think that it did, she would be letting herself in for disaster.

'I'll tell you what,' he smiled, raising himself on one arm to look into her eyes. 'I'll bet you'd like a nice hot shower and a good breakfast. Then we can talk about what to do with this day.'

'You took the words right out of my mouth,' she replied, doing her best to match his own unflappable calm. If he could treat her with such relaxed equanimity, as though nothing had happened which needed to be discussed in any way, then she would do the same for him. Perhaps he was right, after all. What was there to say, or to worry about?

'You look so beautiful lying there,' he said, his eyes caressing her. 'Could a fellow have one kiss to wake up on?'

Her eyes half closed in involuntary rapture as he drew her to him once more. She could not help wondering whether this was the last kiss they were to share. Perhaps their indescribable intimacy of last night was to fall into the category of accidents which occasionally befall good friends, and are soon forgotten by both. If this kiss were the last she must savour it, then, and force herself to suppress her tragic sense that it was already a goodbye.

His lips joined hers, and with an ethereal sweetness he explored the flesh he had known totally a few hours before. Laura felt herself all open to him, all pliant and acceptant, and it was with a great sensation of delighted yielding that she gratefully received the affection he bestowed. If her solitary tryst with Frank Jordan was never to be repeated, she would fix this last kiss in her memory as a secure link to the passion that had been hers in his arms.

Without embarrassment at her nudity or his own, Frank helped her up and watched her move towards the bathroom. She flushed slightly to feel his gaze on her body, and all at once hesitated to meet his eyes.

'Hey,' he called after her. She turned to see him standing with careless grace beside her bed. 'Hurry back.'

Despite their friendliness, his black eyes had never looked so deep, so penetrating.

The phone rang as she was struggling to tear herself away from him.

'Shall I answer it?' Frank asked, looking outrageously calm in his stately nudity.

'No, I'll do it.'

Concealing her shock at the sudden buzz, Laura sat on the edge of the bed and picked up the phone.

'Laura, it's Rob.' The voice was distant, the transmission hollow. 'I hope I didn't wake you up.'

'Not at all, Rob. Is there a problem?'

'Not really. It's about the contract we signed with Pirot. I told Mr Allard yesterday that our lawyers would be in touch about the details, but I forgot to give him the name of the international contract firm we hired to work with him. There's no sense leaving any confusion in his mind. I thought if you were going to be in touch with Pirot today . . .'

'Yes, I intended to call them this morning in any case,' Laura said, her voice catching despite herself as she glanced down at her own nakedness.

'I tried Frank's room, but there was no answer,' Rob's voice added.

For a stunned instant Laura saw herself naked between the powerful man who stood before her and the incisive voice on the line. Feeling atrociously vulnerable and embarrassed, she forced herself to speak in easy, businesslike tones.

'He's right here,' she said. 'We're just on our way to breakfast. Would you like to talk to him about it?'

'No. Just remind him, now that I think of it, to make sure Allard understands the import arrangement on the parts from Syracuse. Tell him to tell Pirot that we're handling the taxes ourselves.'

'Syracuse,' Laura repeated, fixing the word in her mind as she stifled her blushing glance at Frank. If Rob was at all aware of her nervousness, he gave no sign of it. 'All right, Rob. I've got it,' she said. 'See you Monday.'

She hung up the phone with a sigh. All at once she felt ashamed of her predicament. Like a heedless, defenceless girl she sat naked on the bedsheets which had felt the storm of her rapture last night. Yet she was the president of a huge corporation, here in this foreign place on important business . . .

When at last she looked up, Frank was smiling down at her.

'The Syracuse parts,' he said. 'He's worried about the duties.'

She nodded, her slight smile meeting his own.

'You take your shower, young lady,' he said. 'I'll call Allard from my room, and meet you here in ten minutes. All right?'

'All right.'

'And I want you to eat like a horse today,' he added. 'Breakfast, lunch and dinner. My God, what a slender little thing you are. If someone doesn't watch out for you, you're going to waste away to nothing.'

He watched in silence, his arms crossed, as she stood up. Outside the windows the huge city, frigid under its winter wind, teemed with speeding traffic and hurried pedestrians. Laura knew that in an hour or so she would step through the lobby's revolving doors to join that throng of busy people. And she would be on Frank's arm. Her day would undoubtedly hold a bit or two of unfinished business. And after that . . . With a last peek at the rumpled bedclothes beside Frank she wondered if there was a chance they might be lovers again.

'Am I thinking, or wishing?' The question made her blush. As she turned away, its answer quickened in the traitorous glow stealing under her skin.

With teasing persuasion from which all reference to last night's events was banished, Frank convinced Laura to accompany him to the Laurentians for an hour of cross-country skiing after their business with Pirot et Cie. was finished. The trip, past thickly forested mountains in which dozens of ski centres nestled, was like an idyll in a winter wonderland. Despite the rather intense cold, the wind had dissipated, leaving huge banks of snow glistening in the December sun. Threading his way through the Saturday traffic with quiet care, Frank met Laura's eyes with an amused smile.

'Are you sure I'm up to this?' she asked.

'If you can walk, you can cross-country ski,' he laughed. 'It'll do you good.'

To her surprise, he was right. After a few minutes of patient instruction she found that she was able to manage the regular rhythm required to propel herself over the grainy snow. They set off along a well-travelled trail, having memorised the map, and before long found themselves exploring lush forest corridors piled high with soft crystals which exploded as gently as champagne bubbles into the air as their skis slid through them. The stillness of the trails was remarkable after the busy atmosphere of the lodge. No sound broke the silence other than the hushed thrum of their skis. Only the faintest breeze stirred the snow-laden branches of the pines.

The intimacy of the experience was so bewitching that neither felt the need to speak. The woods themselves seemed to conspire to bring them together in this oddly private communication, witnessed by no human eye. Muted calls from nearby trails echoed softly as they approached a crossroads.

Laura felt wonderfully invigorated after her tumultuous night, and thanked Frank for bringing her.

'Cross-country skiing is the one sport for absolutely everyone,' he smiled. 'It doesn't matter how athletic you are, as long as you enjoy the great outdoors. All you have to do is drift along and watch the world pass by. When we get back home we can drive north to Connecticut and do this any time. With all your hard work, it would be just the thing for you.'

Frank must have calculated how long it would take for the route to tire Laura, for she was just beginning to feel a languor in her legs as the lodge came into view once more. After returning their ski equipment, they drank hot toddies before the roaring fire in the lounge. As she glanced at Frank's long limbs stretched before him, Laura could not help letting her eyes rest on him with admiration, and with a secret thrill of possession. That marvellous man's body had been entwined with her own only hours ago, and now she sat beside him as calmly as though he belonged to her.

It was not true, of course, but the fantasy was too intoxicating to banish as she exchanged quiet words with him, watched his easy smile curl his lips as he gazed into the flames, felt him touch her hand.

But as they arose to have a simple, bracing lunch before driving back to Montreal, a disturbing thought overtook her with stunning power. This simple closeness she felt with Frank, so clearly reciprocated on his own side, was part of a sinuous path leading through this sunlit day towards the night. And when the shadows fell at last, and they returned to their hotel for their last hours together before the flight home, what had happened once must surely happen again.

The thought coiled around Laura pitilessly, making her senses tingle with guilty anticipation. She wondered whether she alone was thinking it. Frank's dark eyes betrayed nothing of his feelings. He was every bit as cheerful and self-assured as always, though his demeanour was perhaps a bit more gentle, less exigent, since he deemed this brief vacation essential to Laura's health, and had no intention of renewing his incessant demands for performance until Monday. But could it be that he himself felt the deep, fulfilling afterglow of their intimacy?

Could it be that he would come to her again? That they both knew it, and could no more prevent it than they could prevent the sun from rising tomorrow?

No, she told herself angrily. This evening he would decorously leave her to her sleep, no doubt angry with himself for having taken advantage of her heedless seduction last night, and put the whole episode behind him. He would not wish to hurt her more than he had already. He was probably comparing her charming simplicity in his own mind with the sophisticated wiles of his women friends in New York or elsewhere.

It was already mid-afternoon when they emerged

from their wild expressway and found themselves back in the city. They passed an array of enormous skyscrapers whose bulk concealed countless monuments to French explorations hundreds of years ago. The Nôtre Dame church, gigantic and beautiful, sprang into view as they approached the river. And behind every urban structure Laura saw, the mountain that had given the city its name seemed to loom in its magnificence.

At Frank's suggestion they decided to complete their day with a brief exploration of Centre Town. They walked along Sainte-Catherine Street, with its elegant department stores and crowds of Saturday shoppers, and gazed in the windows of the high-fashion establishments on Sherbrooke Street. Then Frank led Laura into a maze of underground passages lined with shops, restaurants and cinemas, which seemed an entire city under the frozen streets above.

'It's a relief after the cold, isn't it?' Frank asked as he strolled hand in hand with her. 'That's why they built it. Montreal stays cold until late April or so. The snow never melts.'

After returning to their hotel to rest and dress, they took a cab to Crescent Street where Frank introduced Laura to a restaurant which bore an uncanny resemblance to a Paris bistro. Patrons stood at the large zinc bar drinking *demis* of draft beer while waiters in waist aprons and white shirts open at the neck hurried from table to table. The jukebox rang with the sounds of popular French songs.

Laura's active day had given her a good appetite, and Frank watched in humorous approval as she finished the savory onion soup and *entrecôte* he had ordered for her.

'I think this old town agrees with you,' he said as they chose from the cheese tray brought by the waiter. 'Some day, when you're mistress of all you survey, perhaps you'll move Christensen's headquarters up here.'

'It's a thought,' she laughed, weighing his words inwardly. For the first time he had intimated that he truly believed her capable of running Sam's company indefinitely.

But the undercurrent of her thoughts was far more insidious than these bantering exchanges. She could feel the shameless language of her senses sending its lilting phrases into the warm air around her. And an insistent inner voice proclaimed that he, too, must be feeling this secret ferment. The day was almost done. Night was upon them, covering them with its sweet obscurity, drawing them inevitably closer to each other . . .

Bravely Laura tried to match Frank smile for smile, remark for blithe remark, to engage in the easy ebb and flow of conversation for all the world as though his nearness were not sending shudders of forbidden desire through her limbs. It was agony, that performance, and yet it was the only possible way to behave. She dared not admit to herself that in a few more minutes he would say goodnight and leave her alone. But what else could he do? He was too responsible, too much in iron control of himself, to let last night's wild scene repeat itself.

Behind his mask of good humour he must be concernedly asking himself whether this already dependent girl would draw the wrong conclusions from what had happened between them. He must be thinking of a way to let her down gently, so that she would not flatter herself about his future plans. After all, he must continue to work with her every day. Any lovesick airs she might permit herself would certainly make a mess of their business relationship.

She must not embarrass him by throwing herself at him again. It would be too humiliating. She must say goodnight blandly, coolly— just as though she were as adult as he, and knew full well that an unforeseen upsurge of physical need between friends meant less than nothing. She must be businesslike and mature, and let him know that he was still her invaluable adviser and colleague, that she harboured no illusion that he had become her lover, her love . . .

She fought to put everything out of her mind except that one cool moment when she would bid him goodnight and close her door.

As they hurried from their cab into the hotel lobby, bound for the desk where the handsomely dressed clerks awaited, they passed the lounge where she had danced in Frank's arms last night. She sighed to think that he must be sharing her thoughts, for he did not ask her if she would like a nightcap, if she would like to dance. Doubtless he wished her to rest her tired legs after this day of strenuous activity. Perhaps he was tired, and in a hurry to sleep himself. Or perhaps, once he had taken his leave of her, he would go back out to keep a rendezvous with someone.

The crowded lobby and elevator passed as though in a dream, their turbulent sounds banished by her certainty that in five minutes she would be alone in her bed, dreaming pitifully of the man who had shared it with her last night. Let the tears of frustration flow, she told herself, after he had gone. Let her be as silly as she wished in her solitude. As long as she did not throw herself at him again.

Some day she would fall in love and marry, and this episode would persist in her memory as a strange sidelight of this terrible period of eleventh-hour struggles to save Sam's company. It would simply be part of that mad whirlwind of events in which normal rules were suspended by the unexpected. She would live it down, and never speak of it to anyone.

Without a word Frank walked her to her door,

locked his arms warmly around her and kissed her hair. She rested her face against his chest, grateful for this contact which must give her the strength to let him go.

'Thank you for a wonderful day, Frank.'

'Thank you.' His voice was quiet against her hair. 'I'm sorry it's over.'

It was subtle, the movement of his arms that told her he wanted her. Impalpably light, the touch of his palms on her back; and yet never had her body received a message with such stunning force.

There was no time to think twice, nor did she want to. Quietly the door clicked shut, and the shadows enclosed them with an almost conspiratorial softness. Loosened by invisible fingers, Laura's dress seemed to fall away all at once, and she stood in her bra and panties, returning a kiss that sent a shudder of passion through her senses. Her slender hands slipped to Frank's broad shoulders, their passage easing his jacket off before they crept to undo the buttons of his shirt. In a trice she felt the warm skin of his back and hips under her fingertips, smooth and dry.

Their hands must have worked together in a mysterious complicity as she kissed the sinews of his neck, for the whole expanse of his loins fell under her touch with stunning suddenness, the crisp tangle of his man's hair brushing her palms as she caressed him. The last flimsy fabrics came away from her tender flesh, and she stood naked against his firm body, intoxicated by its aroused power.

An instant later she was beside him on the satiny spread, her quiet moan of delight greeting the lips which kissed her breasts, her stomach, her ribs. Had he wished it, she would have given herself to him in that one charged moment, for the wanting that had built up all day inside her was releasing itself in a violent storm. But his caresses were slow, and gently enquiring, as he explored the downy skin he had known last night for the first time.

Exulting in her realisation that he still wanted her, that his own thoughts must have lingered over her image throughout this charmed day, she felt her senses open to him in luxuriant eagerness. Her soft limbs grazed him in their sweet undulations, seeking with a will of their own to excite him. And now there was no embarrassment between them, no diffidence, but only the expanding joy of discovery.

She kissed his eyes, his brow, his hair as he held her closer. His large hands slipped under her back to her hips, and she felt the strength of male fingers capable of lifting her bodily to crush her against him. But she met him delightedly, her knees rubbing his waist, the skin of her legs filling itself with his touch.

Sensing the heat of his man's need, she welcomed it, her hands unafraid to explore him, their fingertips acknowledging and celebrating his desire. A groan stirred in his throat as he pulled her face to his, and she felt herself fairly levitated by the magnetism of him, stunned in air by the lips and tongue that held her.

She would never know whether that entrancing embrace had lasted seconds or long minutes, for even as they touched each other in euphoric release, savouring the novelty of their bodies' intimacy, the terrible momentum of their passion bound them together. In a flash she was his, her arms wrapped around him in ecstasy as every part of her strained to weld itself to him.

She felt his enormous heat gather under her skin, the wild potency of him firing her deliciously, and with a gasp her rapture bestowed itself upon the darkness all around. The past had dissolved vertiginously, and there was no time to think worried thoughts about the future. Only this eternal wave of pleasure existed, this expanding moment, rocking and buoying her forever, forever in his arms.

When at last the storm in their senses had spent itself, it was with an infinite delicacy that his hard grip softened, his embrace grew tender, his firm sinews relaxed around her, warmer and more intimate than ever as the sharp force of him receded, so that she was never bereft of him, never alone.

Her fingers grazed his neck, his broad shoulders with cooling gentleness as she lay under his weight, her body moulded to his own. He kissed her eyes, her cheeks, and the soft scent of her hair suffused him. A tender silence enfolded them both, for it seemed that in that one magical moment nothing in the world had separated them. Perfect oneness had been theirs. And now that it had happened, nothing could take it away.

I love you.

The words stole furtively through her mind, tantalising her at first with their lithe, pretty sound. A little poem in three words, she thought dreamily. And though she knew that in another moment the reality of Frank's separate existence would return to haunt her, she felt an impulse to scoff at it nonetheless. She felt as though she had captured the core of his male essence, known him entirely. A hundred years of living alone could never banish the memory of that moment.

True, the three short words with their burnished, euphonious sound had never passed her lips. But she had known him and, yes, loved him in that burning instant of utter closeness. The dreamed perfection, the fulfilment she had not dared to think possible, was now.

Her body tingled delightfully in his arms as the warm obscurity of the room covered them. She felt him slip the sheet over her nudity and hold her close. Outside the winter wind whirled among the city's steel and granite towers, cruel and vibrant. But here inside one knew the essence of warmth, the purest intimacy.

Minutes passed silently as they held each other, their lips and fingers touching softly. Though stunned into a wondrous languor by the force of her passion, Laura felt no fatigue. Instead, a hidden swirl of excitement, of otherworldly exhilaration flowed through her every nerve.

And as time passed that quick charge of physical joy became indistinguishable from desire's inevitable reawakening. The long arms that held her came alive, the quiet kisses brushing her face grew more urgent, and she knew his passion was rising to meet hers anew.

Again it was perfect, whole and complete, though slower and more dreamlike, the rapture they gave each other. Her sighs coiled around him, and they were sighs of amazement, of delighted astonishment at the pleasure he could bring her. This time she gave herself in sheer bliss, dazzled by the sensations he kindled in her, and by his own responses when her hands crept to touch him, to increase his excitement. Again the mad, luxurious slipping of flesh upon flesh, hotter and hotter, drove her to a height of ecstasy unimagined in her guiltiest fantasies about him. And again he held her in his steadfast embrace, protective and strong, as her gasps whispered in the darkness, and as she relaxed into rapt somnolence in his arms.

She would remember that night forever as an iridescent dream in which fiery explosions of intimacy alternated with long, stunned periods of beautiful rest. How many times she was his she would never know. Whether she had truly slept at all remained a mystery. The night belonged to love, and from it the intervals of everyday time had been banished. For one perfect, endless moment the future had been held off, daunted and outlawed by an immediacy more powerful than the passing hours.

And with each new ecstasy, different from the last, too individual to ever recapture or forget, Laura felt a secret confirmation of the ineffable force that joined her to Frank Jordan.

A change had overtaken her in that enchanted night, and she accepted it in exultation. She would never be the same again. And in that very fact, which, she knew, might expose her to extremities of pain she had never experienced before, she took her pleasure.

For if time retained its cruel power to take Frank away from her forever, it had also brought her this night, whose place in her heart was permanent.

CHAPTER TEN

DAYS later the wintry world of Christensen Products' life-and-death struggle had engulfed Laura again. She was up to her neck in phone calls, blueprints and cost estimates. Frank was again haunting the corridors of Christensen's headquarters like a spirit, his quick glance looking for weaknesses in corporate organisation that might suddenly emerge to thwart Laura's plan to market Molly by late March.

The bespectacled face of Zalman Corey loomed before Laura as the weeks passed, importuning her to be more conservative in her contracting expenses, mutely begging her to be more traditional in her fiscal attitudes. Rob Colwell was in her office often, explaining the uncertain balance of payments governing Molly's parts and assembly, his eyes resting on the reports with the calm of a surgeon whose fingers tie delicate sutures inside the body of a dangerously ill patient. Laura marvelled at his self-possessed confidence in his ability to do messy and difficult jobs with alacrity.

Occasionally a touch of worry clouded his irises as he regarded her, and she wondered whether the secret change which had overtaken her was somehow visible to him. She could not help recalling the discomfort that had found its way into her voice when she had sat naked on the bed in Montreal, only a few feet from her lover, while accepting Rob's instructions over the phone. And she feared that when the three of them were together now at Christensen, her hooded glances at Frank and the tone of her voice in speaking to him betrayed a subtle alchemy that Rob must surely interpret correctly.

She knew that Rob would do anything in the world to protect her, for he considered himself *in loco parentis* and as such had a fatherly concern for her. If he suspected for a moment that her youthful innocence was exposing her to hurts over and above those she had already suffered, wild horses would not prevent him from intervening on her behalf.

On the other hand, his respect for Laura must dictate that he avoid invading her privacy. And so he kept his watchful distance, showing by his supportive demeanour that he was always there if she needed him.

But Laura knew he could not be blind to the profound difference these past weeks had made in her. She could no more conceal the glow of fulfilment in her woman's body than she could hide the firm edge of her newfound confidence.

Frank Jordan had made her a new woman in more ways than one, and she felt that the process was almost complete now. Her lack of conviction in her own competence had taken a back seat to her determination to save Sam's company. She knew who her enemies were, and she felt a professional's visceral certainty that she would prevail against them. The facts and figures at her fingertips combined with the careful strategies in her mind to convince her that victory was attainable.

Each time an obstacle seemed to threaten Molly's marketability, or a financial reversal seemed to make the corporation more vulnerable, Laura no longer wasted time in fear and trembling. She acted. Those around her saw her concentration and her grim commitment. What they could not see was that she had stopped thinking of herself now, and thought only of the job before her.

Laura had become an executive, in her every nerve and sinew.

She alone knew the real secret behind her calm

readiness for bold action. Her private self lived now in a secluded paradise of happiness, and had given up hoping or fearing for the future.

As winter had settled over the country in its cold triumph, Laura travelled its length and breadth with Frank, personally supervising every element of Molly's production. She came to know each mechanical and electrical part of the machine with an almost maternal familiarity, and she questioned her many quality control experts insistently in her effort to pre-empt cost overruns that might menace Molly's affordable price.

Her travels with Frank took her to Chicago, where savage winds roared across Lake Michigan and whirled turbulently through the busy streets of the Loop; and to Bangor, Maine, where icy snow lay in huge piles beside the plowed streets, and the thickly clustered pines seemed to wait patiently for man's era to close so that their roots could buckle the concrete roads and reclaim the land once more. They flew to Baltimore, where winter was a chilly breeze which brought grey days to the charming arrays of row houses whose old-fashioned elegance gave Charles Street its turn-of-the-century look. They drove the pretty parkways through Connecticut and New York to New Jersey, where sodden snow lay among busy factories and enormous oil refineries. They visited Paltron in Massachusetts, where Frank convinced Laura to try downhill skiing with him, and applauded her bravery as she fell flat on her back in the new snow of the beginners' run.

And everywhere they went, their tempered business relationship gave way in the dark of night to the heat of their passion.

Neither said a word about this prohibited undercurrent of their life together. Laura came to feel that she was the possessor of a marvellous, almost mystical secret of which the world remained ignorant. Outside the windows of her hotel rooms the earth was cold, not only in the snow and wind but in the ruthless ambitions of the wilful men against whom her battle was directed. But inside, where no one could see, there was the incomparable warmth and closeness of her endless tryst with Frank.

Each time he touched her in the most casual way, she reflected that his strong hands knew her entirely. Each time she heard him speak, her secret heart told her that those lips knew every part of her. When she saw his muscled body in her outer office, in an airport, a hotel lobby, she knew that other women must be eyeing it with envy. And she knew it was hers.

Only for now? Perhaps.

Not hers alone? Undoubtedly. But Frank was her lover, and nothing could take that away from her.

Lover. The word had taken on an occult, allegorical meaning to her. It signalled their friendship, their respect for each other, and the depth of their intimacy. And above all it bespoke the one truth that she alone possessed, a truth never to be revealed even to Frank: that she had fallen hopelessly and utterly in love with him.

She refused to let herself imagine that the future might make of their affair something more open, more permanent than what it was now. Frank's very silence on the subject confirmed that it could never come to pass. And she had learned to love even that silence, for it acknowledged that their life together was real and beautiful, if only temporary. She shared his reticence gladly, for it brought her closer to him.

He had given her an emerald pendant not long after their return from Montreal, joking that its colour foretold the profits Molly was sure to bring to Christensen Products. She wore it now as a talisman to remind her not only of the rapture she had known

in his arms, but also of the courage he had instilled in
her—a courage which must one day enable her to live
without him.

She lived for the present, grateful for each day, each
night she shared with Frank. The longer their time
lasted, the more secure would be its place in her heart.
The more dizzying the ecstasy he gave her, the more
indelible would be the memory of it.

As they lay together in the shadows, relaxing in the
lovely afterglow of their lovemaking, her eyes and
fingertips lingered in fascination on all the handsome
parts of his perfectly formed body. His dark gaze
caressed her face languorously, and he ran a long
finger through the glimmering strands of her hair.

He could not know that she was taking him in,
filling herself with him in the concentration born of
her understanding that tonight, tomorrow night, the
next night might be the last time she would be his.
She had realised that Frank Jordan was Now. That
was his essence and his magic, and it made all ordinary
modes of experience irrelevant where he was concerned. One could not try to hold him, to keep him, to
second-guess his unseen mind or his unknowable
future. One could not covet him conservatively, the
way one collected assets or prepared a company for
security in years to come.

One could only love him now. And that meant
giving one's love without a thought for oneself. But if
one gave unselfishly enough, renouncing all hope that
he could be tamed and possessed, freeing him to be
the vibrant, uncapturable thing he was through the
very force of one's love, the result was ecstasy.

Yes, she must love him now. But if she loved well,
now would be forever. The future without him could
never harm her.

When the time came, she would marshal her
woman's strength, for which she knew she already

owed him a debt of gratitude, and let him go without a clinging word or a possessive gesture. That would be her final gift to him, and her repayment of her debt. And as he receded into his separate destiny, he would look back on her with respect. In his thoughts he would thank her for her renunciation and approve of her strength of character. She would have shown him in the end that she was indeed made of the tough and durable substance he thought he saw in her when she refused to give up her company without a fight.

So Laura accepted the challenge of her days and the indescribable joy of her nights with a clear mind. She looked upon the past without shame, and upon the future without unrealistic hopes. How could life disappoint her now? She knew a happiness she had never dreamed possible. How could fate wound her? She had no illusions left.

She did not suspect that the very world she viewed with her cautious thoughts could explode into a thousand fragments, like a fragile bubble made of dreams.

It was the last day of February. The hour was late, and Laura was even more exhausted than usual by her day's work. Yet her mood was cheerful, for only three weeks separated Christensen Products from Molly's initial marketing date. The quality control experts in New Haven had passed affirmative judgment on the machine's first mass-produced units, one of which was even now purring unobtrusively in a corner of Sam's office.

Laura was preparing to fill her briefcase with sales projections for study at home when Virginia's amplified voice emerged hollowly from the intercom.

'Miss Christensen, there is a Miss Schell here to see you. She has no appointment, but she says it's quite urgent.'

The name of Schell rang in Laura's ear with a sinister novelty.

'I beg your pardon?' she asked, pressing the button. 'Whom did you say . . .?'

'Miss Julia Schell.'

'All right, Virginia. Send her in.'

Collecting her thoughts quickly, Laura rose to greet her visitor. She recalled having read that the reclusive Julia Bond Schell had no interest in her father's corporate empire. If this were true, what possible reason could she have to call on the president of a company which did not even have a relationship with Schell?

The door opened to reveal a slender young woman whose fine blonde hair was pulled back in a simple chignon. The mauve blouse under her matching skirt and waistcoat was of an exquisite silk, and its colour harmonised beautifully with the amethyst pendant she wore.

Julia Schell's great wealth shone in the very restraint of her clothes and accessories. But it was her delicate and even frail beauty which astonished Laura. The alabaster complexion around her hazel eyes, combined with the slim roundness of her limbs, made her seem a china doll which would shatter if handled too roughly. Yet Laura recalled having read somewhere that Julia Schell was a noted horsewoman. She wondered if this impressive aura of extreme fragility concealed a will as strong as that of Armand Schell himself.

'You're very kind to receive me,' the young woman began. 'I know you must be terribly busy, Miss Christensen, and I'm sorry to burst in on you like this . . .'

'That's perfectly all right,' Laura smiled. 'Please sit down. What can I do for you, Miss Schell?'

The dewy eyes under Julia Schell's long lashes were

troubled as she perched uncomfortably on the edge of the leather chair opposite Laura.

'Well,' she sighed, 'this is very difficult for me, Miss Christensen. Very embarrassing, and ... well, it all may seem far-fetched and ridiculous to you at first. But if you hear me out, I think you'll understand why I felt I had to come to see you.'

She hesitated before going on, and Laura smiled encouragingly, her calculations as to the reason for this unexpected visit well-concealed by her look of calm expectancy.

Julia Schell's hesitancy made her seem more delicate and vulnerable than ever. The tidings she bore seemed to pain her from within, so that she appeared virtually on the edge of tears.

'I might as well come right to the point,' she sighed, 'so as not to waste more of your time than necessary. I believe ... I think you know a man named Frank Jordan.'

'Frank Jordan?' Laura raised an eyebrow in surprise. 'Yes, of course. He's worked for us since just before my father's death.'

Julia Schell nodded, her eyes meeting Laura's with a sort of frightened diffidence.

'Frank Jordan ... is my fiancé,' she said in a small voice.

The effort to contain her shock cost Laura the last of her already spent resources, but somehow she managed to retain the attentive smile which had seemed so natural only a moment ago.

'My father is a man named Armand Schell,' Julia went on. 'He owns a corporation called Schell International, which you've ... probably ...'

'Of course,' Laura smiled. 'Your father's work is known and respected everywhere.'

'Frank Jordan ... works for my father,' the other woman went on in a tone of agonised confession. 'He works for Schell, that is, as what they call a consultant—but I think it's actually more than that. What I mean to say is that he is quite close to my father.'

Laura's heart sank within her breast, and she realised with an inner sigh of despair that the blows her attractive visitor had just struck must now have left visible traces in her eyes.

'And how does this concern me?' she asked, the quaver in her voice belying her measured words.

Julia Schell turned even more pale at Laura's question.

'I . . . don't know much about business,' she said. 'My father and brothers understand corporate life. I've always been the only member of the family who was not involved. But I've been hearing things, Miss Christensen, about Schell International and your company. I know your father died just recently, and I'm very sorry about it. I may be doing the wrong thing, but I felt I had to come . . .'

'What sort of things, Miss Schell?' Laura asked. 'What things have you been hearing?'

'Please call me Julie. All my friends do.' Again a look of paralysed dread stole across the young woman's classic features. 'I overheard a conversation between my father and Frank . . . Frank Jordan. It had something to do with a takeover of Christensen Products, planned for sometime this spring. They were arguing, in a sense, but my impression was that they both agreed on this idea of a merger. Perhaps you already know about this, Miss Christensen. I'm so naive in this area that I'm probably unduly worried.'

'Please go on,' Laura insisted. 'I'd be interested in anything you have to say, and I'll keep it in confidence, of course.'

'Well,' Julie sighed, 'for better or worse, here is what I thought I understood. If I'm not making any sense, don't pay any attention to me. It seemed to me that Frank had been instructed to strengthen your company so that it would not "lose its markets", or something like that. The idea was that a corporate takeover would not be advantageous to Schell International at this moment, while Christensen Products is financially troubled. But Frank's mission in all this—or so it seemed to me—was not to enable your company to resist a takeover by my father . . . by Schell. Quite the contrary. The purpose was to increase Christensen's hold over certain markets, and then to force a merger by applying some sort of pressure on the Stock Exchange. To drive the price of Christensen stock down, using investment specialists . . . to stockpile proxies . . . I'm sorry to be talking over my own head this way, but perhaps you'll understand anyway.'

She pursed her lips in concentration. 'There was a timetable . . . something about March 20th.'

The date of our stockholders' meeting, Laura thought in sudden panic.

'My brother Roy is involved somehow,' Julia added in distress. 'That's what Frank and my father were arguing about. My impression was that Frank's reward for this whole business was to be the presidency of . . . of your company, Miss Christensen. And a free hand in running it. This is apparently not what Roy had in mind, and Frank wanted assurances from my father that he—that Frank—would have his way in the matter.'

'You're saying,' Laura replied, unable to bear another word of the young woman's horrible news, 'that Frank Jordan's actions are for the benefit of Schell International.'

Julie nodded miserably. The fugitive trace of a tear was visible in her eye.

'Frank Jordan is a good man,' she said. 'I wouldn't

be engaged to marry him if he weren't. But the world of corporate finance is a cruel one. I can't escape this awful feeling that my father and his people—including Frank—are planning something that is not in your best interests or those of your company.'

She shook her head with a sigh. 'I'm smart enough to understand what I read about Schell International,' she said darkly. 'The corporation has changed since my brothers took over most of the responsibility. Personally, I don't have the impression that Schell is in business to help people any more, or to make the world a better and more modern place. It's all money and profit and tax losses now.'

Her charming features were twisted by worry as she gazed at Laura.

'I knew your father by reputation,' she went on. 'Christensen is obviously a very fine company. I'm sure you know best how to protect it, Miss Christensen. I'm only here because I received the distinct impression that there was some sort of subterfuge about Frank's involvement with you. Some sort of misrepresentation. If he's trying to make you believe he's helping you, and if his real intention is something else—well, he should be stopped. I can't bear to say this about the man I'm to marry, but there's no choice. Don't believe him, Miss Christensen. Don't . . .'

A sudden sob choked her, and she reached into her small purse for a linen handkerchief.

Thunderstruck by the revelations she had just heard, Laura fought to conceal her emotions. Though her world was falling apart around her, she concentrated her attention on the precise import of Julie's words.

'The intention of the Schell Corporation, then,' she said, 'is to take over Christensen Products late in March, through a stock manipulation.'

Julie nodded. 'If that makes any sense to you,' she said. 'And there was something about a new product . . . An important patent my father wanted to take over for some of his subsidiaries in Europe. They were arguing about that, too.'

Molly, Laura thought, her blood running cold. Her enemies intended to steal Randy's invention for themselves.

The plot in which Frank Jordan was involved clearly had a byzantine complexity. After all, was it not Frank himself who had denounced Andrew Dillon and First Federal as secret cohorts of Schell International? Why had Frank told Laura the actual truth about the bank, rather than to use all his wiles to hide it?

The answer was chillingly simple. Frank had told part of the truth in order to gain Laura's confidence. And his plan had worked. Not only had he convinced her of his own good will, but he had managed to penetrate to the inner sanctum of her own corporate plans, and eventually to influence and control them himself.

Yes, he had told the truth, Laura reflected in panic. But he had left out one critical detail: the fact that he himself also represented Schell International, that he himself was at the core of the plan to take over Christensen Products.

Had she wished to check out his story about collusion between Andrew Dillon and Roy Schell, Laura could have done so. And she would have found that Frank's story was true. Frank, of course, probably expected her to investigate his revelation.

But she had not bothered to do so. She had simply believed him.

And, in her naive innocence, she had ignored the one elementary course of action she should have taken from the beginning: to investigate Frank Jordan himself. A little careful checking would have revealed who he was and whom he worked for. But Laura had simply taken him at his word, taken him into her confidence, followed his advice, on the idiotic assumption that his pretended loyalty to Sam extended to her.

And, when it suited him, she had even taken him into her bed.

'Miss Schell ... Julie,' she said at last, somehow stifling the flood of tears which grew inside her, 'you're very kind to go out of your way to inform me of all this. Please don't feel that you have betrayed your father, or his corporation, or Frank Jordan. I think you have done the right thing, and I'll certainly give careful consideration to what you've told me. Now I think you should put it all out of your mind and concentrate on looking forward to your ... your marriage.'

Julie seemed more forlorn and defenceless than ever as she returned Laura's gaze.

'I ... I feel so sick about all this,' she said. 'If they ... if my father and Frank have done anything to hurt you, please accept my own apology for them. I just hope I've been of help. If everything I've said is nonsense, I hope you'll forgive a silly and ignorant woman for wasting your time.'

She stood up to leave, but hesitated before turning away.

'Frank ... Frank Jordan is an intelligent and knowledgeable man,' she said. 'He is an expert in his field, and a very aggressive executive. What I'm trying to say,' she sighed, 'is that I imagine he can be ruthless in his actions. Oh, I don't suppose I can hold it against him personally. To him, and to all men like him, it's just business. But I felt you must be informed. In my own heart, I—— well, I just don't know what to say.'

Despite her own distress Laura was touched by the figure of utter fragility she saw before her.

'You're right about one thing,' she said, forcing a smile. 'Business is business. We're trained to understand that. I would not blame Frank Jordan for acting on his company's behalf, Julie. And I don't think you should, either. I wish you all the happiness in the world. And please don't let this situation prey on your mind. Thank you for coming.'

Julie hesitated at the doorway, as though unable to tear herself from the moral support of the very woman to whom she had just brought such terrible news. For an instant Laura reflected on what she had read about this delicate young woman. No wonder, she thought, that Julia Schell remained aloof from the corporate world her father dominated. That world would have eaten her alive in a trice. She belonged in a protected environment, far from the machinations of wilful, cunning entrepreneurs.

And soon she would have her gilded cage, under the aegis of Frank Jordan.

With a last pained smile, Julie Schell closed the door behind her and was gone.

The digital clock before Laura showed 5:13. After a moment's thought she hurriedly opened a phone book and found the number she wanted.

'Schell New York,' came a pleasant voice after a single ring. 'One moment, please.'

The silence on the line hung like a pall over Laura's future. If it were all true, she was lost. If one could simply call Frank Jordan at Schell Headquarters, where he was known by one and all as a trusted lieutenant of Armand Schell himself . . .

'Mr Jordan's office,' another voice sounded in Laura's ear.

'Mr Frank Jordan's office?' Laura asked.

'Yes, ma'am,' the secretary answered. 'Who is calling, please?'

'I think I may be a bit confused,' Laura said. 'I left

a message with Mr Jordan's answering service, but I'm not sure he has received it. The service is at 555–1717, isn't it?'

'Yes, that's his personal answering service, ma'am, but they don't forward those messages through us.' There was wariness in the secretary's busy voice, as though she were in the habit of protecting Frank Jordan against unwanted calls.

'I see,' Laura said. 'Well, I'm sure he'll get the message eventually. I won't bother you about it. Thank you very much.'

After replacing the receiver Laura stared blankly at the photos and diplomas on Sam's walls. Though she struggled to prevent all thought from entering her mind, a single damning idea leapt to her lips with fearsome insistence.

I never bothered to check him out.

Like a trusting child she had put herself in his hands. What was worse, she had even presumed to throw herself at him like a starry-eyed adolescent. Eagerly, gratefully she had one his bidding, played the pliant role of his puppet, his Trilby.

And she had flattered herself that the comedy she played had matured her, strengthened her, made her into a real woman and a real executive.

Inside she knew her heart was breaking. Yet she seemed to feel nothing beyond a cold knot in her stomach. She recalled the day of Sam's death, and thanked heaven for the human soul's defensive ability to cover over its deepest wounds with a blessed interval of artificial insensibility. For a matter of minutes, perhaps hours, she would resist the searing pain that must eventually overwhelm her.

During that brief time she must act.

There was much to do, and little hope of success. Nevertheless a sharp, desperate glow of rebellion shot through her veins. Her days of childish passivity were behind her now. And Frank Jordan bore most of the responsibility for that. Very well, then, she thought darkly. Let the woman Frank had created turn upon him now. She would weep her bitter tears over his loss later.

'Virginia,' she said into the intercom. 'Are you still there?'

'Just on my way out,' came the familiar voice. 'Is there anything I can do for you?'

Laura had taken off Frank's emerald pendant and put in a Christensen envelope. Detachedly she watched herself address it to Frank Jordan at Schell's New York headquarters. As luck would have it he was in Manhattan today for a financial meeting, and would not return to New Haven until tomorrow afternoon.

'Get me a standard resignation form,' she said, her finger on the intercom button. 'And call me a messenger before you come in, would you? I have something here that needs hand delivery.'

CHAPTER ELEVEN

LAURA sat in silence, her mind racing, as she waited for Virginia to come in. She knew that action must be taken now, this minute, to save Sam's company. Less than three weeks remained before the stockholders' meeting at which she had planned to announce Molly's distribution to markets all over the country.

Now she knew that that meeting was the intended scene of Schell's takeover of Christensen Products.

In a matter of hours Frank Jordan would know that he had been found out. He would immediately closet himself with Armand Schell or his son Roy and begin planning to hasten the timetable for their assault on her company.

Laura could see the truth in glaring colours now. Andrew Dillon's April 5 deadline for payment of Christensen's short-term notes had been a red herring all along. Schell's real intention had always been to take over Christensen well before that date. The essence of the plan was to drive down the price of Christensen common stock, and force its shareholders to sell in panic, on the very eve of Molly's distribution. Then, when unbearable pressure was applied in a proxy fight by Roy Schell and his allies just as Molly's production expenses had left Christensen Products in an overextended condition, Laura would give in and accept a merger.

The result would be that Schell International would pick up all the marbles overnight and triumphantly market Molly as its own product.

Thus all Laura's frantic efforts to make short-term profits through sales of a brilliant new appliance

would have been in vain, for the attack on her
company would take place before Molly could reach
the marketplace.

Thanks to Frank Jordan's inside knowledge of
Laura's top secret timetable for Molly's distribution.

It was a brilliant, cold-blooded plan, and almost
impossible to thwart.

Laura was so preoccupied by these thoughts that
she did not hear Virginia enter the office.

'The resignation form you asked for,' Viginia said
hesitantly.

Without a word Laura folded the form and sealed it
in the envelope with her pendant.

'I almost forgot to tell you,' Virginia said, her
careworn eyes following Laura's hands, 'you had a call
from Francie Tolliver in Advertising about ten
minutes ago. She said she has urgent good news for
you.'

'Virginia,' Laura said coolly, 'I'm going to need
some help from you tonight. Can you spare the time?'
She pushed the envelope across the desk top without
looking at it.

'Of course,' Virginia replied fearfully. Having seen
Frank's name above the Schell Corporation's New
York address, she eyed the envelope uncomfortably, as
though it were a live thing that might bite her if she
touched it. 'Laura, what's happening? Is it bad?'

'It will be unless we do something. Sit down,
Virginia. I need you to do several things for me.' She
took a deep breath and closed her eyes for an instant in
concentration as Virginia produced her memo pad.

'While you're waiting for the messenger to arrive,'
Laura began, 'I want you to get in touch with Peacock
Associates in Manhattan, and ask for Larry Monk.'

'Larry Monk.' Virginia's arthritic fingers wrote
quickly on the yellow paper.

'If he isn't in his office, find him,' Laura said. 'Tell

his people it's urgent. Have him call me at any hour of the night, right here in the office.'

Larry Monk was a virtual legend in the business community. He was the most experienced and creative proxy solicitor in the country. He and his people were capable of wringing proxy ballots from the most disinterested stockholders in the most remote areas. Laura knew that her first line of defence against a takeover of Christensen was the loyalty of her traditional shareholders. She must convince them not to sell their stock, even if its price began to fluctuate wildly.

'That's number one,' she said. 'After you find him or get the message to him, I want you to find Rob Colwell. Ask him to come here to my office immediately. Then call Michael Sheldon in our legal department. Tell him I'll be here all evening and I'd appreciate it if he would drop in to see me.' Pushing her hair out of her eyes with a nervous finger, Laura pursed her lips anxiously.

'If you can get back to Francie,' she went on, 'tell her I'd like to see her here as well. As soon as possible.'

What am I forgetting? she asked herself desperately. There was not a minute to lose. The slightest oversight could be fatal.

'Now, this is very important,' she said. 'I want you to put all the copies of our stockholders' list in my safe. And all the pre-addressed proxy envelopes. I don't want a single stockholder's name lying around here in plain sight. Can you do that?'

'Of course.' Virginia shook her head in bewilderment. She could not know that the same people who had bugged Laura's conference room were more than capable of burglarising the office for the list of Christensen's stockholders.

Laura cursed herself for not taking that precaution

earlier. Under the law Roy Schell or anyone else had every right to use those addresses to make a tender offer to those thousands of people through the mail. If the offer was as outlandish as Roy's wealth would allow—say, $1.75 or even $2.00 for every dollar of the current value of Christensen's shares, the stockholders would fly in droves to their brokers.

'One other thing,' she added. 'Call our security staff. Tell them that Frank Jordan no longer works for this company. He is not to be admitted to any of our facilities.'

'All right.' Virginia's pained tone made it obvious that her sharp eyes had not missed the telltale signs of Laura's true relationship with Frank. But she kept her speculations under control, for she realised that there was far more at stake tonight than the firing of one executive.

'When all that is done,' Laura said, 'I'd appreciate it if you would run down to the cafeteria and get me a sandwich. I won't dare leave the phone for the next couple of hours.'

A quiet knock came at the door. Virginia answered it on her way out. Rob Colwell entered the office, his overcoat slung over his shoulder.

'Rob,' Laura said, 'I'm glad you stopped by. We have something of a crisis here, and we have to move quickly. We're in danger of being taken over by Schell International or one of its holding companies. We have no choice but to get Molly on the market before our previous deadline.'

'Does Frank know about this?' Bob asked, unbuttoning his jacket as he sat down.

'Frank no longer works for us. I fired him ten minutes ago.' Laura's intent eyes betrayed no emotion. 'I'll explain all that to you at the proper time. What we have to do now is get in touch with all our people around the country and squeeze a week off Molly's schedule. We'll need finished units distributed by March 15th.'

Rob's brow furrowed as he gazed unseeing through the window at New Haven's rainy skyline. He drummed a finger quietly on the arm of his chair.

'Will do,' he said at last, turning back to her. 'I'll get on it tonight.'

Laura nearly sobbed with gratitude to see the unflappable loyalty of the man before her. What she had asked was nearly impossible, and he was prepared to obey without a word. Thank God for Rob!

'Michael Sheldon is coming here tonight,' she said. 'We have to delay the stockholders' meeting by one month, so as to give Molly time to sell before we have to report our earnings. Tomorrow you and Zalman and I will prepare a mailing for the stockholders. It will explain how important Molly is, and will also warn the stockholders that any proposed merger of Christensen with another company will not be in their best interests. There's going to be a manipulation on the Exchange, Rob, and we have to prepare them for it. This has to be the best proxy letter anyone has ever written. I'm trying to get to Larry Monk in New York. He'll know how to help us write it.'

'All right,' Rob said. 'I'll be here.'

'Thank you, Rob. Thank you so much.'

She stood up to see him to the door. Before she could open it he took her in his arms. She felt a terrible weakness in her limbs, and had to fight off the tears of fear and frustration which quickened in her eyes.

'Courage, Laura,' he smiled, his hug warming her. 'You'll make it. We all will. What's life without a little excitement?'

His finger touched her chin as he held her out at arms' length. 'Sam would be awfully proud of you right now,' he smiled. 'As I am.'

Gratefully she returned his smile. A moment later he was gone.

Before she could collect her thoughts the phone rang. It was Larry Monk. By a miracle Virginia had caught him before he left his Manhattan office.

'Okay, Laura,' he said when she had explained her situation. 'You've done the right thing in locking up your shareholders' addresses. Schell will have to take you to court to get them, and that will take five to seven days when the time comes. But here's what I want you to do. Get some people together whom you absolutely trust—and I mean absolutely—and get to work on that list. Is it on a computer printout?'

'Yes.'

'All right. I want you to transfer all the names to three-by-five cards. Typewritten. Name, address, number of shares, and so forth. When you've done that, put the printout in a safety deposit box where no one can get his hands on it. Then simply shuffle the thousands of cards. Make a complete mess of them. Leave them in a cardboard box in your safe.'

'Why, Larry?'

'If Schell and his friends get a court order to force you to turn over the names—and of course they'll succeed—the law does not specify in what *form* you have to turn them over. So what you'll do is to invite them into your office and show them the box of cards. Let them have access to a small xerox machine. It will take them days to copy the cards. If they had the computer list they could make offers to all the shareholders overnight. This way you'll gain a little more time. Hours can count, Laura, so do what I say.'

'I'll do it.' Laura's tired hand wrote furiously on the pad before her.

'Good. Now, delaying your stockholders' meeting is crucial. You were smart to think of it. That month's delay might just save your company. Tomorrow, with your permission, I'll retain Sean Harris to work with your own legal staff. He's the best proxy law specialist around today. He's a good friend of mine, and I'm sure he'll be available to work with us. I'll bring him with me tomorrow. See you when I get there.'

'Great, Larry. Thank you so much.'

Her head spinning as she fought to recall the priorities before her, Laura looked up to see Francie Tolliver standing in her doorway.

'Come on in,' she smiled. 'What's your news?'

Francie swept into the room excitedly, her leather boots gleaming under the attractive skirt she wore. She sat down quickly in the visitors' chair and began rummaging through her purse.

'It's great news,' she said. 'You remember Marva Sims? The movie actress?'

'Flora the maid,' Laura nodded.

'Well,' Francie said, 'I've found her! She's right in New York. She lives in an apartment in Manhattan. I visited her today. Laura, you wouldn't believe her. She doesn't look a day older than she did in that movie. She's bright, alert, and still has all her showbiz instincts, and what's even better, she says retirement has been boring her silly. She'd love to help us out herself with a commercial for Molly.'

'You're sure she's feeling up to it?' Laura pictured Marva Sims in her mind. If she herself associated that angular, intelligent face with a thousand housekeepers, all the older people around the country—homeowners and apartment dwellers—were sure to recognise it.

'She has a touch of rheumatism, but she's absolutely fine. She still belongs to the union and everything.'

'All right.' Laura took a deep breath. 'Time is much shorter than I thought, Francie. I want you to get together with everybody in advertising tomorrow morning. We'll need a perfect script—and I mean perfect—in a matter of days. We're going to run this

Molly ad in regional markets before the product is ready. We'll have to go for advance orders. It won't be easy, Francie, but we must get something on the air right away.'

'No problem,' Francie said eagerly. 'I'll show you a tentative script in a day or so, and we'll work on leasing a studio.'

'And on buying TV time,' Laura said.

When Francie had gone Laura sat in exhausted concentration behind her desk.

Have I done enough? she asked herself desperately, weighing all the contingencies facing her now. When Michael Sheldon arrived she would help him plan anti-trust litigation against Schell in the event of a proposed merger. She did not need Michael to tell her that Christensen would lose the suit. But it would gain time, as would the delay of the stockholders' meeting and Larry's plan to make a deliberate mess of the list of shareholders.

But all those delays could only hold off the inevitable, unless Molly reached the market immediately and earned huge profits.

The situation Laura found herself in was unlike anything she had ever faced before. None of the crises of the last four months could match it for sheer menace. She was alone. She alone must act.

Yet, she realised, in an unconscious way she had been preparing herself for this day since Frank Jordan first warned her about Andrew Dillon and Roy Schell. A thousand little doubts and fears had kept her alert to the possibility of an ultimate danger such as this.

Including remote, tiny doubts about Frank Jordan himself, which she had not had the courage to face consciously.

Frank had been devilishly cunning. At every turn he had eluded her suspicions, gained her confidence. But his one mistake had been to arm her with enough of the truth to arouse her defensive instincts, to sharpen her executive wits.

Now she would use those wits to defeat him.

'I can be cunning, too,' she thought with bitter determination.

Two days later a proxy letter describing Molly's enormous financial promise and the imminent danger to Christensen Products from a rapacious conglomerate was in the mail. The letter urged Christensen's thousands of loyal stockholders to hang onto their shares and, when the delayed stockholders' meeting took place, to vote against a proposed merger. The name and personality of Sam Christensen were mobilised to the hilt in the letter, and it was warned that in the event of a takeover no trace of Sam's guidance of the company towards service and innovation would remain.

Virginia and two trusted members of her own secretarial staff took responsibility for the mailings and for the transfer of the stockholders' names to index cards.

By Friday Laura was in New York with Francie Tolliver and two of her advertising colleagues, poring intently over the tentative script for Molly's television commercial. Seated in a chair beside Francie was Marva Sims.

'As I see this,' Francie said, 'we need Marva to complain to the camera that her employer is too cheap to buy a Molly for his house. Since Marva is the wise housekeeper, she doesn't want to be saddled with the chore of dusting.'

Laura's brow was furrowed in concern.

'I don't think that will work, Francie,' she said. 'Even if we present the millionaire as an eccentric cheapskate, the audience will get the message that Molly costs money—that Molly requires a financial sacrifice. We can't pose the problem that way. The real beauty of the product is that it is so inexpensive. Anyone can afford it.'

'And another thing,' Francie put in. 'So far we don't have any real humour here. Marva can't appear as a mere complainer. We have to underline her character as someone clever, hardheaded . . .'

'Excuse me,' came a diffident voice. Marva Sims was leaning forward in her chair, her friendly eyes fixed on Laura. 'I know I'm just the performer here,' she said, 'and I ought to keep my big mouth shut, but I've just had an idea . . .'

CHAPTER TWELVE

WITHIN ten frantic days of production supervised by Laura herself, a television commercial depicting Marva Sims as a millionaire's household maid was ready to be shown throughout the United States and Canada. Cleverly edited by Laura and her associates so as to communicate a gentle tongue-in-cheek irony, the film showed Marva working in exasperation with a dust rag on her employer's priceless antique furniture, while a narrator's voice deplored the boredom of dusting in general.

What came next had been Marva's own idea, and constituted the real brilliance of the commercial. After a quick cut the camera picked Marva up in her own modest apartment, where a Molly purred in a corner, freeing her from the onus of dusting at home. The simple appliance her employer had been too penurious to buy was clearly well within his maid's own budget.

In the final seconds of the short film Marva was shown in close-up, relaxing with a snack in a rocking chair before a television set on which a football game was in progress. With a wink to the camera Marva abandoned her irascible exterior and smiled for the first time. Her conspiratorial grin, not without its hint of sarcasm over her wealthy employer's cheapness, was a perfect coda to the commercial.

Having been charmed by the witty old actress during the exhausting days of filming she had supervised in New York, Laura viewed the final version of the commercial with some trepidation. But when she saw Marva's impish grin, so perfectly timed and modulated in the final seconds, she felt a thrill of accomplishment. If any advertising message could convince consumers to buy a Molly for their own home, this was it.

As the editors went about preparing 15- and 30-second versions of the commercial for time slots in markets around the country, Laura added her own brainstorm to the film. It was a simple and effective idea, easy to implement. The editors simply altered the image of the football game on Marva's TV screen to show the favourite local team in each region of the country where the commercial was to be run.

Television time had been contracted for in all the major markets for Molly's initial sales drive. Completed by the graphic *'MOLLY: Coming This Month to a Store Near You'*, the commercial went on the air during the second week of March.

Laura and her colleagues sat before their television sets the first evening for all the world as though their personal fates depended on those sixty seconds of film. On tenterhooks they watched as the first half of a popular situation comedy wound towards its end. To Laura's satisfaction the first half of the show was particularly amusing.

'Good,' she thought tensely. 'The audience will be in a good mood. They'll linger in front of the set long enough to see Marva come on.'

At last Marva appeared, instantly recognisable in her familiar role as the sour-faced maid. A hundred old movies came to mind as one looked at her irritable features. Her performance was even more brilliant than Laura had thought initially. When the commercial came to a close she sighed with relief.

Marva Sims had made Molly human.

And now there was nothing to do but wait.

Laura spent the rest of that week beside her office and home telephones, receiving call after call from her marketing division. Sid Ritchie, Christensen's Vice-

President in charge of Sales, became the most important man in her life. She importuned him to inform her of each and every bulk order received for Molly by retailers of any size. She spoke to each and every one of Sid's regional representatives by phone, and was gratified by the immense quantity of advance work they had done on the product's behalf. Each day Sid demonstrated Molly's virtues to visiting buyers from important chain stores, showing off his quality control reports with his accustomed brio.

At first the results were less than encouraging. A large East Coast retailer ordered a cautious 12,000 units of the new appliance, after lengthy negotiations with Sid and his lieutenants. A drug store chain closely associated with one of the Midwest's popular grocery outlets ordered 15,000 units.

In less sinister times, when short-term profit was not a matter of sheer survival, such initial results might have been welcome. But Laura knew that Molly's production and distribution costs, not to mention her unprecedented advertising budget, would outweigh all but the most sensational sales.

Yet with the passing days, as Marva's commercial was repeated around the country and followed up by full-page magazine and newspaper ads, the tide seemed to turn.

By the third Monday in March several important regional department store chains had ordered 80,000 units or more apiece. Not wishing to see themselves outdone, their competitors began to jump on the bandwagon, spurred undoubtedly by telephone queries from consumers about the new product's availability. Discount houses around the nation followed suit.

On Wednesday morning Sid closed a deal with a national mail order house for 200,000 units.

On Thursday the first of the country's best-known department stores shook off its natural inertia and ordered 400,000 units. A nationwide retailer, it commanded respect in the business community for its marketing decisions.

What followed was a deluge. Apparently convinced by their own eyes once they had seen Molly's simple and economical design, the major chain stores in the United States and Canada began beating a path to Laura's door in their haste to take advantage of her product's novelty. Sales of the few thousand units Christensen had been able to deliver already to selected stores were phenomenal.

Molly was a sensation. The retailing community sensed a windfall, and mobilised itself accordingly.

On Friday Sid burst into Laura's office, dragging Zalman Corey behind him.

'A million and a half units, Laura!' he bellowed, his face red with excitement. 'A million five already! And my people can't keep track of all the orders coming in. We've created a monster.'

Laura turned to Zalman, who had opened his briefcase with nervous fingers. She dared not breathe until he spoke.

'According to my calculations,' he said with the barest hint of a smile, 'that puts us over the hump. Well over. If we can get these units out, and if they sell in the stores, the profit will not only wipe out our debt, but we'll have the biggest second and third quarters in the history of the company. At a risk of being hasty, I'd say you've done it, Laura.'

In the next week the most famous retailer in the country contracted to sell Molly under its own name. The deal was closed for 400,000 units with the proviso that the name Molly remained integral to the item.

A dozen offers were made to manufacture more sizeable versions of Molly for stores and offices, with handsome royalties to be paid for use of Christensen's patent.

Contract offers for production of the appliance in Europe and South America were funneled to Laura's legal department.

The response was so overwhelming that Laura felt a pang of worry over Molly's dependability. If the little machine broke down and required servicing, the losses to Christensen under its warranty would be catastrophic. But a glance at the Molly in Sam's office confirmed the quality control experts' enthusiasm. There were no apparent bugs in Randy's ingenious design. The machine functioned perfectly, and Ernst said he had not had to dust the office since it was put in.

Of more concern was the movement in Christensen stock on Wall Street. The first days after Marva's commercial reached the public were disconcerting. Christensen's common stock fluctuated wildly, and trading was so heavy that the Exchange was forced to close it off twice. Laura was convinced that her enemies, having seen the commercial and heard rumours of Molly's promise on the Street, were making their move in a desperate hurry. Each morning she waited anxiously for the financial newspapers, expecting to see full-page ads registering a tender offer to her stockholders.

But the passing days saw a settling of the confusion. The heavy action on Wall Street involved smaller blocks of stock. That could only mean that Molly's success had convinced Christensen's stockholders to hang on to their shares. The wild fluctuations ended, and the price of Christensen common stock began a steady upward climb.

Laura had brought Molly to the public in the nick of time. Her stock was too valuable to sell now. No conglomerator could accumulate a large enough block of it to threaten her.

On March 26th Laura opened the *Wall Street*

Journal to find a half-page public tender offer directed to the stockholders of AMZ Manufacturing, Inc. of New Jersey. AMZ was an important mid-sized corporation which had long been a competitor of Sam Christensen in the machine tool trade.

The tender offer was made in the name of Beta Concepts.

So Roy Schell and his friends had backed off and found another victim, Laura mused with a smile.

On the last day of March Laura received a treacly letter from Andrew Dillon underlining First Federal Bank's many years of service to Christensen Products, and explaining the Bank's reconsideration of its intention to call in the corporation's short-term loans. The letter ended:

> '*We feel that our decades of financial cooperation justify a confidence in Christensen which the Bank unfortunately failed to demonstrate during the sad days following Sam Christensen's tragic demise.*'

The letter amused Laura, for she and her colleagues knew that the short-term debt was meaningless now. The challenge before Christensen Products was expansion, not survival. Laura's long work days were spent in the effort to fill the orders deluging her many plants, and in plans for the acquisition of additional facilities. Within a year Christensen's assets would double, and they must be used to prepare the company for future innovations.

Nevertheless Laura, Rob Colwell and Zalman Corey appeared unannounced at First Federal's Manhattan headquarters the next afternoon. Laura passed through the same corridors and elevators that had been the scene of her initial panic in the wake of Andrew Dillon's threat five long months ago.

Seconds after his secretary announced them, Andrew Dillon hurried from his office, shook their hands warmly and ushered them inside, offering them coffee.

'No, thank you,' Zalman spoke for all three. 'We'll only be a minute.'

Laura watched in silence as he opened his briefcase and took out a large cashier's cheque which he placed on the desk top before Andrew Dillon.

'Twelve million dollars,' Zalman said. 'Penalty interest included. I think you'll find that everything is in order, Mr Dillon. The other short-term notes will be paid in full as they come due in the next few weeks.'

'Well, I . . .' Andrew Dillon stammered. 'This really wasn't necessary. I'm terribly sorry for the inconvenience to you. I thought I had made clear in my letter that the Bank was prepared to extend . . .'

'Miss Christensen prefers it this way,' Zalman said as Laura retained her silence, doing her best all the while to stifle the grin she would have liked to flash in Rob's direction.

'This cheque . . .' Andrew Dillon said.

'Yes,' Zalman interrupted. 'It's drawn on our new account with Concord Bank of Connecticut.. We share your fond memories of our many years of doing business together, Mr Dillon, but Miss Christensen felt a change was in order—in today's changing times. We wish you the best of luck in the future with your other clients.'

A deadly pallor had stolen over Andrew Dillon's distinguished features. He had lost, and he knew it. Not only had his scheme with Schell International failed to produce the hoped-for merger, but he was now losing the account of a corporation whose enormous profits would require expansion that his bank could have financed.

As her colleagues held the door for her, Laura spoke to Andrew Dillon for the first and last time.

'There's always a silver lining, Mr Dillon,' she said. 'At least your bank still owns 50,000 shares of the hottest stock on Wall Street.'

As the door closed behind her Andrew Dillon stood frowning behind his desk.

She had been wrong, he thought ruefully. On instructions from Roy Schell he had sold First Federal's shares in Christensen Products two weeks ago.

CHAPTER THIRTEEN

Two hours later Laura was seated with her colleagues at a large table beside the shimmering drapes adorning one of the tall windows at the Four Seasons restaurant. Beside her were Meg O'Connor and Randy Powers. Francie Tolliver sat next to Zalman. Across the table's opulent expanse, between Rob and Sid Ritchie, was Marva Sims.

No one had had time to think of celebrating during these last hectic weeks. It had been Laura's idea to bring together the inner circle of Molly's creators for a victory dinner, and tonight had seemed the logical occasion.

'Well, what shall we drink to?' Rob asked cheerfully when the waiters had finished pouring champagne.

'To Molly,' Laura smiled.

'To Marva,' Francie said, 'for the best performance of the year in a starring role.'

'To Andrew Dillon,' Zalman suggested with a rare hint of levity. 'He gave us the kick in the pants we needed to get going—and we gave it right back to him.'

'First things first,' Marva said in her quiet voice. 'Here's to Laura. She was the brains behind it all, and the prime mover. I have my own reasons for gratitude toward her, you know. Without Laura I wouldn't have had the chance to work again—and I loved every minute of it. Besides, now that Molly is taking off, I'm looking forward to seeing my face all over the place.'

Laura's eyes rested happily on her friends as she raised her glass. Privately she looked back upon the one important contributor to Molly's success who was not present. Frank Jordan's role in the drama that had led to this happy moment was indeed a crucial one. Perhaps, she reflected ironically, she owed him thanks in the same sense she owed them to Andrew Dillon. Even in his chicanery Frank had spurred her to an achievement of which she would not have thought herself capable.

She found herself returning Rob's quiet smile as these thoughts stole through her mind. Even in his mood of celebration Rob was as restrained and dignified a figure as ever. As she contemplated him Laura could not imagine why he had not married in all these years. The incisiveness of his intelligence, combined with his ruddy, virile good looks, made him an irresistible man. Perhaps, she mused, he was as much a perfectionist about women as he was about his work. Nevertheless, he would one day make someone a marvellous husband.

The sight of his handsome face made her think of the one person, eclipsed now by time and events, to whom Molly's success would have meant so much: Sam Christensen. How poignant to realise that Sam died before the epic struggle of these past months had even begun, and that his death was in fact the calamity which set everything in motion.

In five turbulent months Laura had lost her father, and loved and lost Frank Jordan, whose betrayal she would never be able to forgive. But she had Christensen Products' crisis to thank for the constant challenges that had distracted her from her own hurts. Even now the fatigue and excitement thronging her nerves made grief seem a distant emotion.

Suddenly her reverie was interrupted by a pair of black eyes fixed on her with probing intensity from across the room. For a moment she could not place their familiarity, though the sharpness of their gaze disconcerted her.

Then she realised that the improbable had happened. Frank Jordan was entering the room and had caught sight of her. On his arm was an attractive young woman whose wavy auburn hair set off her friendly eyes to advantage.

In trepidation Laura watched as Frank spoke briefly to the maître d'hôtel and moved toward her. The look in his eyes was neutral as he smiled a greeting to her guests.

'Sorry to bother you all,' he said, placing a hand on Zalman's shoulder as he faced Laura. 'I've been hearing so much about Christensen and Molly that it seemed congratulations were in order.'

He introduced his companion as Helen Rowings. Though everyone obviously knew by now why Laura had fired him, he seemed oblivious to the embarrassment which hung in the air. Thankfully, though, they were in too happy a mood to be impolite. Rob alone seemed poised in dark readiness, his eyes fixed questioningly on Laura.

'And this is Laura,' Frank said to Helen. 'I think we'd all agree that she's the real heroine in all this.'

'I'm so pleased to meet you,' the other woman said, smiling brightly. 'You're quite a story around this town, Miss Christensen. Not many people have handled Roy Schell the way you have, and got away with it.'

'I think our friend Roy may choose his enemies more carefully from now on,' Frank laughed.

'You're very kind,' Laura said with a pained smile. Helen Rowings seemed more attractive with each word she spoke. The gentleness and good humour glowing in her hazel eyes were really quite seductive. Sighing inwardly, Laura thought of unfortunate Julie Schell. Her fiancé was clearly dallying with yet another woman behind her back. Laura herself had evidently been neither the first nor the last.

A moment later they had gone. Despite her best effort to feel only bitter triumph on seeing Frank Jordan, Laura was tormented by the sense of loss his appearance had stirred within her. The sight of his sharp eyes resting on her in simple admiration, without a hint of anger or defeat, had disturbed her. He was a good loser, at least. One could say that for him.

But that warmth in his regard had brought back haunting memories of their many bewitching evenings together, absorbed in each other's company inside hotels and offices while the winter wind raged outside in any of a dozen cities. It all came back in a fearsome rush, and the cold knot of indifference Laura had coveted inside herself these last weeks was softening into a hollow of grief that wrenched her heart. She had not succeeded, after all, in accepting the inevitable philosophically when time came between her and Frank Jordan. She would never forgive him for his treachery, but she knew she would never be able to forget him either.

As he disappeared around a corner with Helen on his arm Laura wondered if she had seen him for the last time in this life. The thought sent shocks of pain through the corners of her mind whose existence she had tried to deny for many weeks.

She did her best to contribute to the mood of levity which continued throughout dinner, but she did not have the courage to accompany her friends on the night on the town to which they were looking forward. Gently refusing Rob's offer to take her back to New Haven, she sent them all on their way with her best wishes and took a cab to Penn Station for the train home.

An hour and a half later she was alone in her apartment, dressed in her bathrobe, contemplating the Franz Kline watercolour which Sam had loved.

'Every corner of it tells a story,' he had often said, 'if you look at it long enough.'

But tonight the abstract swirls of black and grey spoke only of loss.

Though Laura had wanted to be alone with the feelings warring inside her, the solitude of the apartment did not seem to help. She sat on her couch in silence, waiting patiently for the flood of tears that had never come since she had learned the truth about Frank. But even now an inner defence held stubborn sway over the tide of pain which rose and fell in waves within her.

She could feel the strength in her veins. Tomorrow she would be at her father's desk, where a photo of Sam himself had replaced that of Laura. An interviewer and photographer from a national women's magazine had an appointment with her at two o'clock, and they were merely the latest in a series of visitors from the media. Laura was a celebrity.

'Then why do I feel like a lonely little girl?' she asked herself, her legs curled under her in the shadows. 'A miserable, heartbroken wallflower whose date has just invited someone else to the prom . . .'

The buzzer sounded suddenly at eleven-thirty. Laura supposed it was Rob, concerned about her abrupt change of mood in the wake of Frank's unexpected appearance. Grateful as she was for his protectiveness, she wished he had not bothered to come. He could not help her now.

She stepped back a pace in involuntary terror as the door opened to reveal Frank Jordan's tall form in the shadowed hallway. The look in his eyes was frightening. She could see powerful emotion in his black irises, along with an almost superhuman effort to control that emotion.

'What are you doing here?' she asked, gathering her bathrobe around her.

'I'm sorry to disturb you,' he said. 'I can see you're getting ready for bed.'

Despite herself she watched unmoving as he closed the door behind him. The suppressed violence in his demeanour made him seem unspeakably imposing in his dark business suit.

'I'll be honest with you,' he said. 'After we said hello tonight, I couldn't help wondering whether that was the last time I'd ever see you again. I didn't have the chance to say what I would have liked to say, in front of all those people, so something told me I should come to find you.'

'All right,' she returned coldly. 'Say it.'

'I want you to know,' he said, 'that there are no hard feelings about anything. You did a great job with your company, and now you have the success you deserve. I understand why you did what you did . . .'

'You understand,' she repeated bitterly.

'Yes,' he insisted. 'It was the only reasonable course. We couldn't go on forever the way we were. But I'd like to tell you how much I . . . enjoyed it while it lasted.'

'Enjoyed it!' she said, her anger threatening to overwhelm her. 'Well, that's wonderful for you, Frank. I'm glad it was a pleasure for you.'

'It was,' he responded simply. 'It was something I'll never forget. If it hurt you, I'm sorry.'

She stared at him, weighing his arrogance in wonderment. He spoke of the past as though it had been a honeymoon, rather than a betrayal.

'All's well that ends well,' she said ironically. 'Since you're so worried about hard feelings, you might tell Roy Schell the next time you have lunch with him that all is forgiven now that the best man has won.'

Perplexity vied with the odd intensity in his black irises.

'Speaking of that family,' she added sharply, 'I

think perhaps you ought to be running along now, Frank. I'm sure your friend Julie must be worried about you. Which is understandable, to judge from your companion at the Four Seasons tonight. Your life seems to involve quite a few strands to keep track of. A real juggling act, so to speak.'

The reproachful words had tumbled out before she could stop them, and she cursed the grain of jealousy they contained. But the dangerous light flickering in his dark regard remained clouded by incomprehension.

'I don't get it,' he said. 'You seem to have me mixed up with the wrong people.'

She laughed bitterly. 'Do I? Well, never mind, Frank. It's late, and I have work to do tomorrow. I don't have time for your self-justifications.'

He had advanced upon her slowly as she spoke, and towered over her now. For an instant she recalled the daunting image of his tall frame in Sam's darkened office, the night he had first warned her about Andrew Dillon. His threatening posture, so virile and erect, had left its mark on her senses for weeks afterwards. Now she knew it had all been part of his own plan to betray her.

'If you're trying to blame me for something,' he said, 'you might as well come out with it.'

'Blame you? Never, Frank. You did what your instincts told you to do. Perhaps, in your own way, you saw no harm in it. Why don't we just leave it at that?'

He shook his head. 'I can see it's worse than I thought,' he said. 'I'm sorry, Laura. But your company is back on its feet again. I'm glad of that, at least.'

'No thanks to you,' she shot back, a black rage overtaking her as she regarded this complacent stranger, so foreign, so hated, who nevertheless carried an irretrievable part of her woman's heart in him, and would take it wherever his destiny led him.

Her words must have pushed him over an unseen edge, for he grasped her slender arms convulsively, his large hands like iron manacles.

'What's that supposed to mean?' he asked, his voice low, his lips close to her face.

'Take your hands off me,' she hissed, struggling ineffectually in his grip. 'Get out of here.'

'I can't leave it like this,' he said. 'I wanted to help you, not hurt you.'

'Tell that to Julie,' she said, tears of frustration coming to her eyes. 'I'm sure she'd be interested to know that your motives are so exalted.'

'Why do you mention her?' he asked. 'She's nothing to me.'

'Good for you,' she said, hurting her wrists as she writhed against him. 'She'd love to hear that. I'm sure the same goes for Helen. You're quite the ladies' man . . .'

'Listen to me,' he warned, a terrible urgency in his voice. 'A lot of things have come between us. More than I thought, I suppose. But don't ever talk to me about other women. You're . . .'

All at once he hesitated, suppressing his own words with tight control. She felt the tremendous force of him, coiled upon itself so close to her in the charged air of the room, and cursed herself for having let him in.

'You're wrong,' he said at last.

'Liar,' she retorted in dark triumph.

With stunning suddenness he pulled her against him, the power of his arms forcing the breath out of her. Her angry struggles had loosened the tie of her robe, and to her horror she felt the crisp cloth of his jacket against her naked breasts. The earthy male scent of him, palpable under his elegant clothes, suffused her as he forced her lips open. Madly she squirmed to get away from him, but so tight was his grip that her efforts succeeded only in forcing her nudity to rub itself jerkily against his hard body. In a trice his kiss had penetrated her, his tongue caressed her own, and she realised in panic that there was no place to hide from him.

She did not know what he was trying to prove in his angry way, but she was horrified by her own response to him, for already, in her every sense and sinew, she felt tantalisingly at home in his arms, at home in this tense embrace which held her soft flesh to the firmness of his muscled limbs.

Fiercely his hands furled the warm terrycloth which hung about her in disarray, pulling it up, forcing it aside so that they could close around the gentle curve of her thighs, her hips. They were hands that knew every inch of her, every secret corner which had awakened to the ecstasy of love for the first time under his touch. And as she fought against him, aghast at the intimacy of his hold on her, the sly rhythm of her old passion was stealing over her naked skin, binding her ever closer to him, making her shudder with inviting female undulations, wanting and loving this bondage that infuriated her.

He was turning back the clock in that wild instant, abetted by her own flesh and soul, and she could not think how to stop him. The taunting heat inside her expanded dizzyingly as he pulled her hips to his own. She felt the hard force of him against the silken nudity of her limbs, and the taut tips of her swollen breasts quickened against his deep chest as his tongue slid over her own, lithe and knowing. All at once his anger seemed gone, eclipsed by a passion to which she was even more vulnerable. His fingers were on her back, her shoulders, the soft skin beneath her waist, alive with wanting, their touch a triumphant greeting after painful weeks of separation.

She was his woman, those warm caresses seemed to say. The strong woman he had fashioned from a self-conscious girl, and whose needs could only be satisfied by this man who was already part of her, too deeply rooted inside her to excise and banish, whatever his unforgivable perfidy. Well might she struggle, in her bitterness, to break the chains that bound her to him. Her very strength had come from him. She was fighting against herself, and her squirming could only lead her inevitably to his bed, and to the hard man's flesh that had known her eager caresses and gaze of fascination so many times.

But he hesitated, as though shocked by the fury of his own need, and withdrew his kiss without relinquishing his iron hold on her. His hand furled her sleek hair with a sort of awed enquiry as his gaze took in the swollen shadow of desire in her features. He himself seemed amazed by the occult power of this intimacy which joined him to her, by the very softness which clung involuntarily to him, the vulnerable female flesh he fondled. With a slowness born of unseen emotions he kissed her temple, her earlobe, her neck, his lips grazing her skin with indescribable familiarity.

The gentleness of those sweet kisses tore at the heart of her resistance to him, and when the hot flare of his need brought him to part her lips once more, and his groan of desire filled her senses like a deep caress, she thought she was lost. She felt her own fingers slip over the hard ripples of muscle under his shirt, traitorous fingers which longed to slide around his hips to the crisp hair on his chest, his stomach, to pull gently at his belt until it opened, to pleasure him like a pliant slave who knew that she could never be whole without him, that no price was too high to pay for the ecstasy he alone could give her.

But a saving impulse, from the depths of her mind

and heart, forced her to grasp him suddenly in an embrace of entreaty, and to speak the only words that might stem the tide of his passion.

'Don't,' she whispered. 'You'll kill me.'

The words had slipped out with a will of their own, and in an instant struck their mark. She knew that at the very centre of his lovemaking had always been a wellspring of respect, a willingness to bring her pleasure while refusing to violate her. Though his cruelty had known no limits in the treachery he plotted behind her back, he would not dare use his body as a weapon to torment her.

'Go now,' she heard herself say in a voice that beseeched and commanded. 'Never come back.'

And as he released her, it seemed that she could at last find her anger once more, and defend herself at the price of a heart broken by her own refusal.

'I never want to see you again,' she said, avoiding his eyes as she pulled the bathrobe around her with a shudder. 'Go away and live your life, Frank. Please.'

Her gaze was fixed on the shadows covering the walls. Awed by the finality of her own words, she fought to survive her last instants in his presence. Never again would she look into those black eyes behind which paradise had seemed to open upon her, unbearably delightful. Never again would she hold those warm hands, feel the caress of the wry smile which had buoyed her spirits when she felt so alone, touch the tanned skin whose virile fragrance had charmed her nights.

She heard him turn and walk away. The door closed upon him with a hushed brutality that made her feel faint. For a brief moment a hard inner voice congratulated her on the remnant of strength that had forced him away.

Then, in a tide that washed away all thought, her tears came at last to torment and comfort her. For what seemed an eternity she sat alone, quiet sobs shaking her breast, hot tears inundating her.

When at last she dried her eyes and hurried to her bed, she was a changed woman. The future opened out before her, calm and serene in its indifference. She felt that the metamorphosis which had begun the day of Sam's death was now complete. She was a hollow shell, and would remain so.

Life beckoned her to new challenges, and she intended to meet them. But in her expectancy there was no hope. Tomorrow her work would offer blessed distraction from this emptiness which, she knew, would never be filled again. Her heart belonged to a stranger, and she must now go about the bleak business of living in exile from her very self.

CHAPTER FOURTEEN

IT was May. Winter had long since given way to a rainy spring on the East Coast, and finally a few days of fresh sunshine were arriving to signal summer's eventual advent.

The face of Laura Christensen had become familiar on the pages of dozens of business publications. Her courageous and clever stewardship of Sam Christensen's company to unheard of prosperity was a story the media could not resist. Features on her had appeared in women's magazines all over the country, and she had even been asked for TV and radio interviews. Her selection as Businesswoman of the Year was a virtual certainty.

To Laura's relief her college graduation portrait had finally been eclipsed in the press by a recent photo which showed her as she was today: dressed in a simple suit, her sleek hair pinned back, her smile touched by diffidence and a trace of fatigue.

Molly's sales had grown apace since the first hectic weeks of production, and Laura was up to her neck in judicious expansion plans for Christensen. There were factories to buy and lease, related product lines to design and develop, materials to buy, and companies to acquire. Christensen Products today was a far richer company than the one Sam had left Laura, and she was resisting considerable pressure to move its headquarters to Manhattan.

Laura had never worked for fame, and the attention she was receiving made her uneasy. To her astonishment, it showed no sign of subsiding, for her youth and beauty, once such an obstacle to recognition of her abilities, were now a journalist's dream come true.

But in recent days a single story had eclipsed all others in the business press. Armand Schell had died after a long illness, leaving his empire in the control of his sons and their allies. A host of dignitaries from governments around the world had attended his funeral in Manhattan. In a lengthy eulogy one of the President's cabinet advisers, himself a former Schell employee, had praised Armand Schell's contributions to America in war and in peacetime.

The press teemed with stories about the power struggles destined to shake the Schell conglomerate. It was known that Roy and Anton Schell had no intention of sharing power amicably, for only their father's presence had kept them from each other's throats during his lifetime. Of concern also was the enormous political leverage that had died with Armand Schell. His corporation had not lost a single important anti-trust suit in the last forty years, for no government dared incur his displeasure. With Armand dead, the questionable acquisitions Schell was involved in around the globe might no longer go unchallenged.

Laura had read this news with interest, not only because Schell's acquisition of AMZ Manufacturing brought its influence close to Christensen's own markets, but because she wondered where Frank Jordan would fit into the new scheme of things. She also wondered sadly whether his planned marriage to Julie Schell would soon become a reality. Though the welcome coldness in her emotions prevented her from dwelling morbidly on the prospect, she could not help scanning the business and social columns for news of the wedding.

But these thoughts were far from her mind one Saturday morning when she found herself on Fifth Avenue in Manhattan. She had come to buy clothes, for her wardrobe was pitifully inadequate now that her responsibility required her attendance at so many formal functions.

Summer in New Haven would be hot as always, and Laura was in search of some comfortable suits and dresses. Fifth Avenue was particularly attractive in the bright morning sun and, having ordered all her purchases to be delivered to her new and larger apartment in New Haven, Laura was strolling happily, unencumbered by bags or boxes, when a familiar face flashed across her vision.

She turned to see Helen Rowings beside her on the sidewalk. Helen also had stopped in her tracks, and was smiling.

'Remember me?' she asked. 'Of course I didn't have any trouble recognising you, Miss Christensen, with your face all over the papers.'

'How are you?' Laura asked, her friendliness covering over her acute awareness of the other woman's relationship with Frank Jordan.

'Oh, fine,' Helen smiled. 'Work, work, work. I imagine you're swamped yourself, with Molly doing so great in the stores.'

'I'm doing the best I can,' Laura laughed. 'It can be a grind.'

Helen hesitated, and seemed to be making an inward decision.

'I don't suppose you'd have a minute for a cup of coffee,' she asked. 'Now that I see you, there's something that I'd appreciate talking to you about.'

Laura glanced at her watch. 'All right,' she said, intrigued despite herself by Helen's invitation.

A few moments later they were seated in the corner booth of a busy coffee shop.

'You're nice to take the time,' Helen said, her friendly eyes regarding Laura. 'I probably shouldn't be bringing any of this up to you. It's on the confidential side, to tell the truth, and Frank would have my hide if he knew.'

Laura said nothing, but hid her irritation at the mention of Frank's name behind a polite smile. Despite her pangs of jealousy she could not help liking Helen's gentle, down-to-earth manner and self-effacing wit. No wonder, she thought, that Frank hesitated between a creature of porcelain delicacy like Julie Schell and this fine, attractive young woman.

'It's all ancient history to you now, I'm sure,' Helen began. 'But from my position on the sidelines, I couldn't get rid of the feeling that there were some things you didn't know about Frank when you knew him—and when you fired him.'

I knew enough, Laura thought bitterly.

'You're right,' she said aloud. 'It is ancient history now.'

'Nevertheless,' Helen said, 'I hope you'll lend an ear for a moment. If what I have to say is old news, fine. If not, it might just interest you. Believe me, I'm not trying to interfere. If I hadn't bumped into you on the street just now, I never would have dared get in touch with you.'

She took a deep breath. 'I've known Frank for about five years now,' she said. 'I met him when I went to work for Schell as a junior executive. He had already been there for three years or so, and was quite a celebrity. He was Armand Schell's right-hand man, and everybody could see how brilliant he was. The rumours were all over the place about his future role in the corporation, and how he would handle Roy and Anton, and so on.'

She hesitated as the waitress brought their coffee. Laura could see the concentration in her attractive features.

'I'm getting ahead of myself already,' Helen smiled. 'Schell was not a fun place to work, and that's putting it mildly. But Frank was the head man where my section was concerned, and he, at least, liked my work and tried to encourage me. We used to play tennis sometimes—mixed doubles with a married couple from my floor—and Frank would take me out to lunch occasionally.'

She shook her head with an amused laugh. 'Of course, Frank is an incredibly handsome guy,' she said, 'but I never had any illusions about romantic possibilities where he was concerned. In the first place, I'm just not his type, and I knew it. He was a good friend, and I was satisfied with that. But most importantly, the accepted wisdom around Schell was that Frank was practically engaged to Julie Schell—Armand's daughter—and that he would marry her someday and assume an awful lot of power within the corporation.'

She looked at Laura. 'Here's where it gets interesting,' she said. 'People at Schell were so in awe of Frank that they didn't dare tease him about Julie. But I had become friendly enough with him that I took the plunge one day and asked him about her. His reaction amazed me. He was very angry. Not at me, but at Julie and her father. He told me that after his first year at Schell, he had become very close to Armand. Now, during that period the "old man", as we called him, was already becoming rather retiring, and losing his hold on the business. Meanwhile, he had this daughter by his second marriage—which ended in divorce—and he didn't know what to do with her because he was already so old. She was a shy girl, quite reclusive, and he felt guilty about the divorce. So he asked Frank, as a personal favour, to pay some attention to the girl, because she was so lonely.'

Laura listened in silence, weighing Helen's words carefully.

'That's where the rumours started,' Helen went on.

'People saw Frank with Julie at company functions, saw the two of them with Armand when he appeared in public, and drew the logical conclusion. It was supposed to be a relationship made in heaven. Lonely heiress and handsome executive—all that.

'But what people didn't know was that Frank couldn't bear Julie. That's what he told me the day we spoke of it. He said that her china-doll sweetness was nothing but an elaborate front for the outside world to see, and that underneath she was every bit as ruthless a person as her brothers.'

She smiled. 'That amazed me, of course,' she said. 'But Frank explained how Julie had taken advantage of Armand's guilt about her mother, and had him absolutely wrapped around her little finger. Armand Schell himself! Stranger things have happened, I guess. Now, Frank was annoyed enough already at playing escort to Julie when she needed a date. But as time passed he began to realise that she had more ambitious designs on him. What she wanted, he said, was to marry him someday, and see him outstrip her brothers for control of Schell International.'

Seeing Laura's raised eyebrow, she nodded. 'Don't laugh,' she said. 'The idea was within the realms of possibility, because Armand trusted Frank more than his own sons. The only fly in the ointment was that Frank couldn't stand Julie, and was already looking for a way out of the company. The point is that Julie was a realist as well as a schemer. She knew how to take advantage of people's weaknesses. No one but Frank realised how ambitious she really was, and is.'

She frowned.. 'I soon found out for myself about Julie Schell's influence,' she said. 'One day I was fired by an ax man from Personnel, without an explanation. Of course I was upset, but also relieved in a way, because Schell was such an unpleasant environment. They helped me find another job—thank heaven for small favours—and I thought no more about it. Then, one day last autumn, Frank showed up at the accounting firm where I worked, and told me he had also left Schell. I couldn't believe it. He was giving up so much!'

She sighed. 'Then he dropped a bombshell. My firing had upset him, and he had talked to Armand Schell about it. To make a long story short, he wormed out of the old man the fact that he himself had had me fired, for the craziest reason: his daughter was jealous of me! Apparently Julie had heard about my friendship with Frank and overreacted to it. So she wheedled the old man into getting rid of me.'

A bitter laugh escaped her lips. 'Well, that was it for Frank. He had seen Schell International turning into a corporate snake pit during his years there, and this was the last straw. He could laugh off Julie's designs on him, but not her actions. He saw through her enough to know that there was nothing romantic about her attitude. Power was all she wanted from Frank. But she saw me as a threat, so she had me removed from the picture.'

Her eyes rested gently on Laura. 'Frank knew your father by reputation,' she went on, 'and loved the idea of working with him. His only concession to Armand was to retain his consultant's position long enough to see through the projects he had controlled over the previous years. He asked me whether he could help me find a better job, because he felt personally responsible for what had happened to me. I said I was happy enough where I was. We both laughed a lot that day, because "Hell International", as we called it, was finally behind us.'

Laura sat in silence, shocked by what she had heard. If Helen was telling the truth, the lovely young woman who had so tearfully denounced Frank Jordan to her in Sam's office was not only a dangerous schemer, but also a brilliant actress.

'Now, Laura—may I call you Laura?' Helen asked.

'Of course,' Laura smiled.

'Now, I think I've given you the overall picture. I'm not going to pry into your own affairs, because it's none of my business. I don't know why you fired Frank, and I don't have to know. I saw him a couple of times during the months he was with you, and he was terribly excited about your work. He considered Christensen a breath of fresh air after eight years at Schell.'

Her brow furrowed in concentration, Helen seemed to search for words to express her thought. 'Let me put it this way,' she said. 'Julie Schell lost a great deal when Frank walked out on her and her father. Frank was her only chance for the influence she wanted, and, like all the Schells, she wasn't in the habit of taking no for an answer. I truly believe she was actually jealous of me. Not out of love, but out of ambition. If she is really the sort of woman I think she is, her need for revenge would go deep. She wouldn't want Frank to be happy anywhere else—or with anyone else—and she'd act on that basis.'

Laura had turned pale at her words, and Helen was looking at her curiously.

'Did I strike a nerve?' she asked. 'I'm sorry, but . . .'

'No, never mind, Helen,' Laura said. 'It's just that . . . well, if what you're saying is true, I may have made a big mistake.'

'Laura,' Helen said, touching her hand, 'Frank would kill me if he knew I was telling you this, but I can't help it. I heard him talk about you when he was at Christensen, and I saw the look in his eyes the night we ran into you at the Four Seasons. It was a look I had never seen before. I know Frank, and I know you meant something very special to him. If I thought the long arm of Julie Schell had succeeded in coming between you two . . .'

The truth was coiled pitilessly around Laura. In the last year her credulity had brought her close to disaster on more than one occasion. First she had taken Andrew Dillon at his word when he threatened her with bankruptcy. Then she accepted Frank's version of events without checking out his own background.

And finally, she had taken Julie Schell's accusations at face value, without establishing their validity on her own.

One fact emerged now in a new light. In the end, Christensen Products had actually been saved from bankruptcy or takeover. But had it been saved by Laura alone? Was it not Frank whose advice had been the driving force behind the strategies whose ultimate success was now touted in the newspapers? Were not Frank's initial warnings about Roy Schell the key to everything?

If Helen was telling the truth, Julie had been diabolically clever. She had simply denounced Frank in the vaguest possible terms, using information she could easily have gleaned from any of a dozen sources about Christensen's dangers. She might have known of her own knowledge that her brother wished to acquire Christensen. All she had to tell Laura was that Frank himself was implicated in the plan.

And Laura had believed it all, and had fired Frank without asking him to explain.

'Let me ask you something,' she said to Helen. 'Did Frank ever mention a proposed takeover of Christensen Products by Schell?'

'By Armand Schell?' Helen shook her head. 'Impossible. The old man was through with acquisitions by the time Frank came to Schell. That would be Roy's game, or Anton's. It was their little competition. Each one would take over companies unilaterally, and use his own power on the Board to force through the mergers. If Roy acquired an electronics company in Maryland, Anton would do the same in Brazil or Belgium. It was that crazy policy that turned Schell into the mess it is today. But Armand himself was out of that part of the business. All he ever did was entertain heads of state and work on his memoirs.'

'If someone at Schell was interested in Christensen,' Laura asked, 'would Frank know about it?'

'Nothing escaped Frank when he was still with the company,' Helen said. 'Afterwards, I don't know. But I'll tell you one thing, Laura. If he did know of a takeover plan when he was at Christensen, he would have done everything in his power to stop it. He hates Roy Schell and his brother, and all they stand for.'

Laura shook her head in an agony of indecision. She recalled the words Frank had spoken the night he had come to her apartment.

I wanted to help you, not hurt you.

If Helen was right about everything, it was easy to understand why Frank had seemed perplexed by Laura's angry remarks about his relations with Roy and Julie Schell.

Why do you mention her? he had said. *She's nothing to me.*

You seem to have me mixed up with the wrong people.

But why then had Frank accepted Laura's firing of him without saying a word in his own defence? If his efforts on her behalf had been sincere, he should have been furious at being fired.

Furious, and deeply hurt . . .

A decision began to take shape in Laura's mind, irrevocable and urgent.

'Where is Frank?' she asked abruptly.

'In Nassau,' Helen said. 'That's where he lives since he left you. As a matter of fact, that's the end of the story. He finally convinced me to leave my accounting firm and go to work for him. He's a

consultant to several big corporations. But he can't
stand the Coast any more, so he stays in the Bahamas
while I act as his liaison. I fly down there once every
three weeks or so to go over things with him.'

Helen hesitated, her lips pursed. 'I'm going to open
my big mouth for the last time, Laura,' she said. 'He's
not happy there. He's closed in on himself, and I'm
worried about him. If it has anything to do with you
. . . well, I don't know what to say.'

'Is he there now?' Laura asked. 'Today?'

'I assume so,' Helen replied. 'He was here last week
for Armand's funeral. For old times' sake, he said. I
haven't seen him since, but I'm in constant touch with
his answering service. If he went anywhere, I think I'd
know about it.'

'Have you got his address?' Laura asked, seized by
an impulse she could not control. She must get to the
bottom of her relationship with Frank Jordan now,
today. And in order to do so she must see him in the
flesh.

Helen's integrity was too obvious to give rise to
suspicion. She must be telling the truth. And if she
was, Laura had not only fired the man whose every
effort had been on her behalf for four months, but she
had told him to his face that she never wanted to see
him again.

She dared not allow herself to hope that her
personal relationship with him might be saved. But
she could not live with the idea that she had rejected
him on the basis of the accusations of the scheming
woman who had already made his life miserable at
Schell.

Laura did not allow herself second thoughts. She
took Frank's address from Helen, thanked her quickly
and expressed her hope that they would meet again
soon. Then she hurried to the nearest telephone to call
her travel agent in New Haven. A reservation was

booked for her on the next flight from Laguardia to Nassau. She informed her answering service that she could be contacted at Frank's address, and took a cab to the airport.

An hour and half later she was on a non-stop flight to Nassau. She had no extra clothes with her, and had not even thought to bring any personal effects. If she stayed the night she would buy whatever she needed. She had to see Frank.

As the plane soared high above the Atlantic Laura turned the facts over and over in her mind. There was no doubt about it: Frank's actions had all been consistent with the idea that he wanted to help her. And in fact he had succeeded.

But how had Julie known when to denounce Frank? How had she known which weapon would strike at the heart of Laura's trust in him? Why had Frank not defended himself the night he came unannounced to Laura's apartment?

There were too many questions. Closing her eyes, Laura tried to put all thought out of her mind.

But one idea hammered insistently at her. Julie Schell's story of her engagement to Frank had destroyed a gloriously intimate relationship on which Laura had placed a thousand unspoken hopes. That had been the cruelest blow of all.

And even now an impish voice inside her wondered out loud whether there was the slightest chance that Frank still cared for her. She banished the thought desperately. She had been hurt too often in the past year to entertain absurd dreams about the future.

She had loved him once. Now she intended to clear the air with him, and apologise if apologies were in order. That was all.

It was late afternoon. Outside the window Laura could see the sun descending slowly towards the horizon. The captain's amplified voice pointed out

Grand Bahama Island below. Laura could see catamarans and sailboats in the water near beaches which glowed like crescent moons in the golden light.

New Providence came into view minutes later as the plane descended. Possessed by a terrible urgency, Laura did not hear the stewards' welcoming words. Though she had never seen these beautiful islands, they were merely a bland background for her final destination.

Tiny Nassau International Airport flashed quickly before her eyes as she hurried towards the taxis and buses waiting to pick up arriving passengers. The tropical air was delightfully scented with the fragrance of sea and flowers. A smiling cab driver whose white teeth gleamed against his brown skin in the afternoon light nodded amiably after a glance at the address Laura showed him. He whistled soundlessly as the cab drove along the left side of the street past groves of trees festooned with bougainvillaea, hibiscus and oleander.

The cab left the inland airport and soon reached the coast road. Limestone houses with wide verandahs and overhanging upper porches passed by, their windows protected by louvres from the glare of the setting sun.

His intuition having told him Laura was a stranger to the islands, the driver pointed out the many cays along the horizon. Laura was momentarily charmed out of her reverie by the sight of a flamingo strutting calmly on a deserted beach—the only such bird she had seen outside of a zoo in her whole life.

No wonder, she thought, that Frank had chosen such a lovely place to live in solitude, far from the rush of Manhattan.

Tactfully the driver avoided asking Laura whether she was here on business or for pleasure, or for a visit. Had he done so she would not have known how to answer him.

The sunset was beginning to spread its fiery spectacle across the entire sky as the driver slowed to a stop beside an isolated mailbox. After peering at it for a moment he edged the cab into a narrow dirt road which descended toward the ocean.

A lengthy trek through dense foliage led at last to a circular drive beside a comfortable house nestled under tall trees. The thump of the surf was clearly audible from behind it. Though the sky was still bright, the thick leaves cast dark shadows over the drive. It would soon be night, and Laura had made no plans at all for a hotel reservation or even transportation. Momentarily unnerved by her impulsive arrival in this far-flung place, she had to steel herself to see her plan through.

A jeep was in the driveway. Behind it stood a small sports car. Laura wondered abruptly whether Frank was alone here, and whether her appearance might interrupt a business or social meeting, or perhaps something more intimate. She began to regret her spontaneous decision to come, and had to recall Helen's assurances in order to give herself courage.

After paying the driver she took a deep breath, walked to the door and rang the doorbell. A muted tinkle sounded inside the house. For a moment she heard nothing else. Perhaps Frank was outside on the beach.

At last soft steps were audible behind the door. With a hollow click the latch came loose. The door opened slowly.

Laura's heart nearly stopped.

Julie Schell stood before her, dressed only in a man's bathrobe, her delicate eyebrow arched in surprise.

'Miss Christensen,' she said calmly. 'What a surprise. Do come in.'

CHAPTER FIFTEEN

In a state of shock Laura entered the house. Its lean, attractive furnishings passed before her eyes in a blur. Behind a large picture window the surf fell heavily against a lovely little beach. A sandbar brightened the water a few yards from shore.

'Frank isn't in just now,' Julie was saying. 'He's in town. Would you like something to drink?'

'No, thanks,' Laura said, her breath catching in her throat. 'I mean yes. Whatever you have.'

'We have soda, fruit juices, all kinds of alcohol—whatever you like,' Julie said with a proprietary shrug. 'Frank likes to keep the place well stocked.'

'A glass of soda would be fine,' Laura said, perching uncomfortably on the edge of a handsome wicker chair. 'Miss Schell, I'm . . . I was terribly sorry to hear about your father. Please accept my sympathy.'

'That's nice of you,' Julie said without emotion, moving unhurriedly in her bare feet toward the kitchen. Her silvery blonde hair was splayed in careless waves over the robe she wore. 'It wasn't unexpected, of course,' she called back, 'but we were all shocked nonetheless.'

A moment later she emerged with a tall frosted glass and placed it on the table beside Laura.

'I didn't realise you were coming,' she said. 'Frank is great to be with, but he can forget to tell me the most basic things. Is it business?'

'Yes,' Laura stammered, feeling a flush of embarrassment come over her in the warm air. Though a lovely breeze furled the curtains beside the window, the atmosphere seemed unbearably claustrophobic.

Julie lounged comfortably on the couch, apparently unperturbed to be seen in her nudity. Her demeanour was far from that of the diffident, frightened girl who had visited Laura in Sam's office. There was a palpable hardness in her beautifully rounded limbs, her voice, and above all the clear eyes that regarded Laura.

'Actually,' Laura admitted, 'Frank wasn't expecting me. I'm terribly sorry to burst in on you like this. It was some business I wanted to discuss with him. Something rather urgent. I suppose I should have called.'

'Not at all,' Julie laughed. 'We're very informal here.' She seemed determined to present herself as the mistress of the house, and Laura dared not ask whether she herself was visiting Frank. In pained perplexity she tried to think of something to say.

'It's beautiful here,' she said at last in a wan voice.

'Yes, isn't it?' the reclining girl answered with a quick glance toward the beach. 'A romantic setting. Just the thing for Frank.'

Laura wished she could find a way to get up and leave gracefully, for the absurdity of her position was coming home to her with increasing force. She had invaded the privacy of a couple which could scarcely welcome her. She cursed the impulse that had made her take Helen at her word about Frank.

'So Frank doesn't know you're coming,' Julie smiled coolly.

Laura shook her head.

'I wouldn't want to be presumptuous, Miss Christensen,' Julie said. 'If you're serious about being here on urgent business, that's well and good. I thought I understood that you and Frank were no longer one. In any case, I might suggest that if your business is personal, you may have made your trip for nothing.'

The venom in her words was unmistakable. Laura's embarrassment was reaching a fever pitch. But something in Julie's ill-concealed cruelty struck a strange note, and she resolved to hear her out.

'I'm not sure I understand,' she said with studied neutrality.

'I suppose we shouldn't talk behind Frank's back,' Julie sighed, 'but he makes no secret of his many . . . involvements. He is a very masculine man, and, to put it bluntly, a promiscuous one. It's the nature of the beast, and one has to forgive it. I did long ago. I do think, though, that it would be tragic for any of his acquaintances to assume his flings are any more than just that.'

Laura said nothing. She knew her emotions were colouring her face. Her impulse to come here seemed to have brought her straight into the maw of Frank Jordan's sinister life. But no matter what happened now, she decided, she would do what she came here to do. She would not leave before finding out exactly where the truth about Frank lay.

'I can forgive him a lot,' Julie went on. 'I decided years ago that the advantages of being with him outweighed the disadvantages. And I know the feeling is mutual, because Frank never strays far. My poor father wanted us to marry before his passing, but neither Frank nor I felt the time was right. I enjoy my own independence, and Frank . . . well, Frank would like to get the wild oats out of his system before we settle down and raise a family. I can't really blame him, you see. It's a purely physical thing, after all. He and I see eye to eye in so many ways. We really knew we were made for each other when we first met. Birds of a feather, as they say.'

'I'm happy for you,' Laura said with a forced smile. 'But this doesn't concern me. As I said, my visit is on business.'

'As you like,' the other woman said, getting up with a sigh. 'I thought it might interest you to know where things stand. I'll be back in a moment.'

With a distinctly contemptuous turn of her head she walked from the room.

Moments passed in atrocious silence, accented by the hushed boom of the surf outside. The cry of a sea bird echoed distantly. Laura could hear a clock ticking somewhere in the house.

Her misfortune was almost farcical, she reflected as she sat alone by the window. Julie had taken cruel pleasure in treating her like a lovesick woman scorned who had flown here in a desperate attempt to regain her lover's affections. And was there not, in fact, a terrible grain of truth in that notion? In her guilty heart Laura had dared to hope that more than her professional friendship with Frank Jordan might be saved today.

Why, she wondered, had Helen lied about Frank's involvement with Julie? Why had she made such a capricious effort to plead for him, behind his back? Perhaps Helen felt that Julie was bad for Frank, and had decided on a mad whim to play matchmaker by propitiating Laura. Or perhaps Helen's motives were as inscrutable as those of everyone else in Frank's life.

Nevertheless, Helen's description of Julie's character seemed amply borne out by the spiteful display Laura had just witnessed.

Even now she heard a radio turned on somewhere in the house. Julie was obviously content to let her visitor stew alone while she went about her business.

A single question remained: was Frank innocent of involvement in the plot that had nearly destroyed Christensen Products?

'What difference does it make?' Laura thought miserably. If Frank were innocent, her apologies could hardly interest him now. Her firing of him was undoubtedly ancient history in his mind, as was their short-lived affair.

In humiliation she wondered what to do. Her pride dictated that she call a cab and return home immediately. But the prospect of embarrassing herself further, and confirming Julie's suspicion about the reason for her visit, immobilised her. She could not sit here like a fool, waiting for Frank to come home to his mistress. Neither could she bring herself to turn tail and flee.

After what seemed an eternity of silent waiting she prepared to find Julie and ask to use the phone. The crunch of automobile tyres on the gravel outside stopped her in her tracks.

So the worst was to happen, she thought. Frank was here. She would have to play this painful comedy through to the end.

To her surprise the doorbell rang. Julie emerged nonchalantly from the bedroom wing, still clad in Frank's bathrobe, and walked to the door without a glance at Laura.

What she saw when she opened it must have surprised her, for she stepped back a pace and watched in silence as a man entered the room.

For the second time Laura turned white in shock.

It was Rob Colwell.

Ignoring Julie, he advanced upon Laura, his expression grim.

'Rob,' she exclaimed. 'What are you doing here?'

'It's all right, Laura,' he said. 'Your answering service gave me this address. I may be out of line, but I thought I could help.'

Her first impulse was to fly to him as her saviour. Steadfast and loyal as always, he was here at her service. He could take her home, take her away from this miasma of ominous intrigue surrounding Frank Jordan.

'Rob,' she said, 'I'm at a loss. I don't understand.'

'Where's Jordan?' he asked, wary determination in his eyes.

'He's not home,' she replied.

'You haven't seen him?'

She shook her head. He shot a dark glance at Julie, who was standing in the doorway, a speculative look on her face.

'Come with me now, Laura,' he said in a low voice. 'I don't know what possessed you to come here like this, but this man Jordan and his friends are no good for you. Hasn't he done enough to you already?'

'Rob,' Laura asked, still trying to collect her thoughts, 'what made you come all this way? Why are you here?'

'I came to stop you from doing something stupid, Laura. I don't want to see you hurt more than you have been already. What business could you possibly have with Jordan after what he's done to you?'

Laura stared at him in confusion. Every sinew in her body longed to cling to Rob for protection now, and to let him take her away from this strange outpost in which she felt so defenceless. But the very idea that he would have rushed here the minute he found this address seemed out of character for him.

Nevertheless her second thoughts could not compete with Julie's cruel revelations. The hopes Helen had raised in her were dead now. The best course was to leave with Rob and try to forget Frank Jordan's alien world. She must leave it behind her forever.

Only this morning she had been a confident young woman, proud of her work and content with her existence, as she shopped on Fifth Avenue. And now here she was, a few short hours later, trapped like a victim in a foreign clime, the tentacles of Frank's endlessly jarring existence wrapped around her. Rob offered a quick, clean route of escape.

'All right,' she said, rising to her feet. 'Let's go, then.'

Rob took her hand with a smile. She prepared to give Julie a lame excuse for their departure.

Before she could find the words, the sound of a car stopping came once more from the driveway.

All three stopped in their tracks, their glances darting from each other to the darkness behind the screen door. Quick footsteps sounded in the gravel outside.

Dressed in tan slacks and a t-shirt which hugged his deep chest, Frank Jordan entered his house with long strides. He frowned to see Julie's déshabillé, and looked quickly from Rob to Laura.

The words he spoke were like a knell of catastrophe over Laura's whole world.

'I don't think I have to introduce Mr Colwell and Miss Schell,' he said with a hard smile. 'I believe they know each other already.'

A stunned silence hung in the air. The four people in the room stood uncomforably, unseen forces raging among them. Julie's glance at Rob was irritable. Rob avoided Laura's shocked gaze. Having spoken his unexpected words, Frank had eyes only for Laura, their expression darkly probing.

'Get your clothes on, Julie,' he said at length. 'There's someone here to take you home.' Though he did not bother to look at her, the command in his voice was so imperious that she hurried towards the bedrooms.

'Laura is leaving with me,' Rob said, finding his voice at last. His face was red with anger. 'If you stand in her way, Frank, or bother her again, I'll kill you.'

'She didn't come here with you, did she?' Frank asked, ignoring the other man's threat. Laura shook her head.

'Then you'll decide for yourself, won't you?' he told her grimly. 'You came here to see me, and you're going to see me.'

All at once the robust energy that had seemed part and parcel of Rob Colwell's male essence appeared to dissipate. He stood in the middle of the living room, his eyes turned now towards the darkening ocean outside, oddly crestfallen and deflated.

Laura turned back to Frank in utter bewilderment. He had not moved from his place by the door. Though his powerful limbs were tensed for action, he seemed determined not to approach Laura, but to speak his piece from a distance.

'I spent a lot of hours wondering why you fired me the way you did, so suddenly,' he said. 'I knew it had to be something that had nothing to do with my work for you. Something outside. The only clue I had was that you sent your messenger to my office at Schell. But, in the end, that clue was enough. I knew someone from Schell must have gone to you behind my back and misrepresented me to you. Since I was already through with Schell forever, there was only one person who fitted the bill. It couldn't be Armand, because he and I understood each other. It couldn't be Roy or Anton because they were both delighted to see me go.'

He crossed his arms, his eyes never leaving Laura.

'It had to be Julie,' he said. 'I recognised her style. Always behind the scenes, always conniving. But a question remained. Julie knew I would never come back to Schell. She knew that as well as Armand did. So what did she have to gain by compromising me with my new employer? Not much. Would she frame me out of pure perversity? I don't think so. Not unless she found out somehow that my relationship with you was more than that of employee to employer. That would make sense. Julie could never bring me back to Schell, but she could do her damndest to see that I was never happy with another woman.'

Laura stared at the long lines of his implacable

man's body, hardened by anger and by his iron control of himself. He was a terrifying sight, and an indescribably handsome one.

'But Julie couldn't know how I felt about you,' he went on. 'Not unless someone told her. Someone who was in daily contact with both of us. Someone who could see that the looks passing between us were those of a man and a woman. Someone who had a reason, a personal reason, to want to kill that relationship at all costs. Someone who cared so much that the very sight of us together was more than he could bear. Only one man was in that position.'

His eyes left Laura to dart a glance at Rob, whose back was now turned as though in ineffectual defence against the blows struck by Frank's words.

'He had to act,' Frank went on, 'but he couldn't risk trumping something up against me himself. That would make him look bad in your eyes, Laura. A friend should never be the bearer of bad news. So he did some checking and found out that someone already existed who was more than motivated to come between us, and guileful enough to do so efficiently. Julie Schell. He contacted her, no doubt in an apparently accidental way, and let her understand that I was involved with Sam's daughter. Then he sat back and waited. In a matter of days she made her move, and I was fired.

'As it turned out,' he said, 'your company was saved after all, and he must have been delighted. Frank Jordan was out of the picture, and the status quo had been restored. Until you ran into Helen Rowings today in Manhattan and flew down here. When he heard about that, he rushed to stop you, and almost succeeded.'

Laura had sat down in a daze, shattered by Frank's words. Rob was staring out at the waves, his eyes bleak and empty.

'I wouldn't blame him too much, Laura,' Frank

said. 'He did what he did out of love. He was loyal to Sam Christensen and to his company, and he was a big enough man not to feel threatened when I was hired. He knew his value. I don't think he even felt betrayed when you took my advice over his about First Federal. He's a professional, and wanted what was best for you. But his world fell apart when the woman he had loved and waited for since she was a teenager chose a stranger named Frank Jordan to love, instead of him. That was the last straw.'

Laura watched in horror as Rob turned and walked from the house without a word. The screen door closed quietly behind him, its clink a fatal sound thrown over her entire past.

An engine burst into life outside. A moment later its hum was receding into the trees, drowned by the thrum of the surf.

'Why did you . . .?' Laura asked in a breathless voice.

'Let him get away with it?' Frank smiled bitterly. 'I thought you belonged to him, Laura. I thought you two had an understanding, with Sam's blessing. I knew how he felt about you the first day I came to work for Sam. I could see it in his eyes. I considered myself the fifth wheel in the whole picture, since I had just come on the scene from another company.'

He shrugged. 'I was head over heels in love with you from the first moment I saw you,' he said. 'And I'm afraid my jealousy made me behave a little coldly toward you, those first weeks. I couldn't resist you, and I was sure you loved someone else. Well, that night in Montreal, and afterwards . . .'

He exhaled sharply, as though the memory were too intense to bear.

'As I say,' he went on, 'I couldn't resist you. You were so beautiful, such a woman . . . But I couldn't bear to put any strings on you. That's why I behaved as though nothing had happened between us. When you did the same, I assumed it was because you loved Colwell all along. I felt guilty as hell for taking advantage of you behind his back, but I told myself you weren't a schoolgirl. You were a woman, and knew what you wanted.'

An infinite sadness had stolen into his black eyes.

'At least,' he said, 'I tried to make myself believe that. All along I worried that I was hurting you, tearing you . . . In the end I gave up on the future and tried to hang on to the present, for as long as it might last. It ended when you fired me, of course. The best idea seemed to bow out gracefully, even though I suspected there was something behind that pendant wrapped around my resignation form. Whether you blamed me for what we did together, or never cared at all, the result was the same.'

A tender smile curled his lips as he went on. 'Besides,' he said, 'I knew by then that you were strong enough, and smart enough, to see your company through without any more help from me. I had served my purpose. And you and Sam had restored a lot of my faith in human nature after eight years in that Schell snake pit. I knew I would never be the same without you, but I was damned proud of you, Laura, and proud to have known you. I had the memories of our time together . . . They say it's better to have loved and lost than never to have loved at all. I just prayed to God that I hadn't hurt you . . .'

A movement in the hallway interrupted him. Fighting her impulse to throw her arms around him, Laura watched in silence as Julie Schell returned from the bedrooms, her suitcase in her hand, a look of malignant anger in her limpid eyes.

Frank went to the screen door and motioned with an upraised hand. Steps sounded on the gravel outside, and a man Laura had never seen before entered the room. He was dressed in a finely tailored business suit, and the hint of grey at his temples made him look particularly distinguished. But as he stood between Frank and Julie, Laura gazed in awed fascination at his eyes. They were the coldest, most inhuman eyes she had ever seen.

All at once a spark of recognition made her glance from the stranger to Julie.

'Roy Schell,' Frank said neutrally. 'Laura Christensen.'

'Come, Julia,' the other man said after a hard, evaluative glance at Laura. 'We're going home.'

He took Julie's suitcase and held the door open for her. Hatred and defeat mingled in her eyes as she darted a look from Laura to Frank. Then, with a shrug of contempt, she strode out the door, her head held high.

At last Frank sat down. His eyes scanned the ocean. Laura regarded him in silence, her nerves racing.

'Julie cornered me at Armand's funeral,' he said, 'and begged me to let her fly down here for a few days. She said she was depressed and needed to think. I let her come—out of regard for the old man, I suppose. He had really loved her after all. That's why he let her get away with so much.'

His smile was rueful. 'It was my mistake,' he said. 'As soon as she got here I could see she felt no grief over his death. Her kind can't feel a thing like that. She just wanted to see what I was up to. I think she wondered whether I had a woman here.'

With a sign he locked his hands behind his head. 'After a decent interval,' he went on, 'I had it out with her about you and Christensen. She admitted what she had done, in a flood of phony tears, and threatened to harm herself in some way if I kicked her out. Comical as that idea was, I believed her capable of just about anything, so I called Roy in Manhattan. I told him if he didn't get on one of his private jets and get the hell down here to take his sister out of my hair, I would make use of a few things I know about his financial dealings of the last few years.'

He laughed. 'That made him jump,' he said, 'because with the old man dead the government is going to be a lot less pliant where Schell International is concerned. I was waiting to pick him up when I got Helen's message that she had talked to you and that you might be on your way here. That's why I was a little late getting back. When I walked in here and saw you with Colwell, I wasn't sure what to think. But when I found out you hadn't come together, I knew I had been right about him all along.'

He turned to look at Laura, his dark gaze alive with passionate enquiry.

'Now he's gone, Laura,' he said, 'and you're still sitting here. Was I right about you?'

Tears had quickened in Laura's eyes as she listened to his words. For months, unbeknownst to her, Frank had been feeling the same pain, the same longing that had tormented her unmercifully. He too had clung to the present in his belief that the future was sure to separate him from her, and had seen his worst fears confirmed when she exiled him violently from her life.

Now he sat a few feet from her, unable to convince himself that time had truly brought her back to him. Could it be, she asked herself in wonder, that only those few feet of mere space now stood between her and the man whose place in her heart was more permanent than life itself?

'I loved you, Frank,' she said quietly. 'I . . . love you.'

Tears blinded her as the words came free at last, the dream they carried shimmering unseen in the darkened room. Her woman's soul leapt within her breast, delivered at last of the burden it had suffered and cherished alone for so long, and she thought she would die to see that secret fly from her, triumphant in the night, towards the stranger she loved.

But his arms had encircled her, warm and protective as home itself, and she heard the words on his lips now, a whisper that stole through all the corners of her past, banishing their pain as it opened her to a future beyond her hopes.

'I love you, Laura.'

She felt his smile as he kissed away her tears.

'Laura Jordan,' he said. 'How does that sound?'

The gemlike syllables stunned her in their novelty, for she had never dared to say the name to herself. Yet it was natural and beautiful, like a charmed destiny that had waited long years for her steps to lead her to it.

For an answer she hugged him to her with hands that seemed to discover him for the first time, dazzled by the firm reality of these handsome limbs which would recede from her no more.

The hushed rhythm of the distant surf conspired softly with the long arms that cradled her in the darkness. She let herself rest at last in this wordless intimacy which seemed to grow and flower with each passing instant. Strong and sure were those steadfast arms, and eternal as the waves the time which opened before her now.

She tried to recall the young woman whose impassioned gaze had scanned the sleeping limbs of the man she loved, forcing herself at every moment to give him up even as the very sight of him filled her heart to overflowing. He was Now, she had told herself. That was his essence, and her agony, for she dared not hope to belong to him.

But already that young woman was slipping quietly from her memory, along with the anguished days and private tears she had endured with all her courage.

Yes, she mused. Frank was Now.

And Now was forever.

An epic novel of exotic rituals
and the lure of the Upper Amazon

THE TAKERS
RIVER OF GOLD

JERRY AND S.A. AHERN

THE TAKERS are the intrepid Josh Culhane and the seductive Mary Mulrooney. These two adventurers launch an incredible journey into the Brazilian rain forest. Far upriver, the jungle yields its deepest secret—the lost city of the Amazon warrior women!

THE TAKERS series is making publishing history. Awarded *The Romantic Times* first prize for High Adventure in 1984, the opening book in the series was hailed by *The Romantic Times* as "the next trend in romance writing and reading. Highly recommended!"

Jerry and S.A. Ahern have never been better!

TAK-3